OPERATION CRIMSON STORM

Selected Borgo Press Books by ROBERT REGINALD

Academentia: A Future Dystopia
Ancestral Voices: An Anthology of Early Science Fiction
Ancient Hauntings (ed. with Douglas Menville)
The Attempted Assassination of John F. Kennedy
BP 300: A Bibliography of the Borgo Press, 1976-1998
Choice Words: Writers Writing About Writing (editor)
Classics of Fantastic Literature (with Douglas Menville)
Codex Derynianus III (with Katherine Kurtz)
The Dark-Haired Man; or, The Hieromonk's Tale (NE #1)
Dreamers of Dreams (ed. with Douglas Menville)
The Exiled Prince; or, The Archquisitor's Tale (NE #2)
Forgotten Fantasy: Issues #1-5 (ed. with Douglas Menville)
The Fourth Elephant's Egg; or, The Hypatomancer's Tale (#4)
"A Glorious Death": The Human-Knacker War, Book Three
The House of the Burgesses (with Mary A. Burgess)
If J.F.K. Had Lived (with Jeffrey M. Elliot)
Invasion! Earth vs. the Aliens (War of Two Worlds #1)
The Judgment of the Gods and Other Verdicts of History
King Solomon's Children (ed. with Douglas Menville)
Knack' Attack: A Tale of the Human-Knacker War (Book Two)
The Martians Strike Back! (War of Two Worlds #3)
The Nasty Gnomes: A Novel of the Phantom Detective (#2)
Operation Crimson Storm (War of Two Worlds #2)
The Paperback Show Murders
Phantasmagoria (ed. with Douglas Menville)
The Phantom's Phantom: A Novel of the Phantom Detective—#1
Quæstiones; or, The Protopresbyter's Tale (Nova Europa #3)
R.I.P. (ed. with Douglas Menville)
The Spectre Bridegroom and Other Horrors (ed. with Menville)
They (ed. with Douglas Menville)
Trilobite Dreams; or, The Autodidact's Tale: An Autobiography
Worlds of Never (ed. with Douglas Menville)
Xenograffiti: Essays on Fantastic Literature

OPERATION CRIMSON STORM

WAR OF TWO WORLDS, BOOK TWO

ROBERT REGINALD

THE BORGO PRESS

MMXI

OPERATION CRIMSON STORM

DEDICATION

To the Memory of

Liz Fishman
(3 March 1942 - 28 January 2005)

And the Road Not Taken,

y por

Decano César Caballero

"Amigo viejo, tocino, y vino añejo..."

AUTHOR'S NOTE

Despite the plethora of indications to the contrary on the Internet, this Borgo Press edition is the first separate publication of this novel, which has only previously been issued as part of the omnibus edition, *Invasion! Earth vs. the Aliens* (2007). The novel was announced for publication by Underwood Books in the Fall of 2005 under the title, *Operation Crimson Storm*; covers were created for same, and orders were solicited, but for a variety of reasons beyond the publisher's control, the book never actually appeared then. Ironically, if the first book in the sequence, *War of Two Worlds* (as it was then titled), and its sequel, *Operation Crimson Storm*, *had* appeared on schedule, the third book in the trilogy, *The Martians Strike Back!*, might never have been written, since its fate was dependent on sales of the first two volumes. And so it goes!

—Robert Reginald
23 February 2011

CONTENTS

PART ONE
MARS ASCENDANT

Thou art the Mars of Malcontents.
—William Shakespeare

This is the way the world ends
Not with a bang but a whimper.
—T. S. Eliot

CHAPTER ONE
WALKING ON EGGS

You can't make an omelet without breaking some eggs.
—Old French Proverb

GEOFF ALEXANDER, 8 JULY, EARTH YEAR MCMXCV
TETON COUNTY, MONTANA, PLANET EARTH

I've been coming here to Teton County for, oh, eight summers now, looking for the Holy Grail of dinosaurs. The landscape hereabouts could best be described as "burnt-orange." Everything is seared by the sun. The fields dry up, the streams run low, and the dust permeates your clothing, your eyes, and even the ice chests. Daylight lasts a good fifteen or sixteen hours this time of the year, and at times seems to burn its way right through your skull. Everyone takes it slow and easy at the digs, from the greenest novice to the brown-tanned veteran. "Sweat" labor is the operative word. No one gets paid much of anything for digging up bones, but it sure as hell beats just about any other activity that I can think of.

We'd been on site for a month already, excavating a hadrosaurus nest from the late Cretaceous period, within a million years or so of the great event that'd killed off all the big beasties in sixty-five and one-half million BCE. Duck-billed dinosaur eggshells and nesting sites are pretty common 'round here, as are fossils of the critters themselves. They must have roamed the area in huge numbers during the Age of Reptiles. They sure as hell left enough remains, from bones to coprolites, to fill a dozen museums.

I was taking a break from the heat and bugs about one in the afternoon, drinking a cold beer and munching on some chips, when Rowena San Diego sat down next to me.

"Hey, Dr. Alexander, Dr. Alver's got something he wants to show you," she said.

"What?" I asked.

I'd just found a comfortable place to sit, and really wasn't inclined to move.

"Dunno. He just said it was real urgent like. I mean, you're the boss man here."

Boss man, indeed! All that means is that I'm responsible for securing the equipment, getting permission from the property owners, arranging for transportation, making sure we have ample medical kits, food and drink, portable chairs, radios, tools, *etc., etc., etc.* And I won't even talk about the paperwork.

"OK," I said.

I finished the brew and headed over to the South Forty.

"What've you got, Duke?" I asked.

Alver stood up. He was a short, middle-aged man with a paunch and balding skull, but he had a nose for fossils like no one else I ever met, and he could also do a "Chipmunks" version of "Take Me Out to the Ballgame" that I swear had everyone in stitches within seconds. Women found him irresistibly attractive, for some strange and terrible reason.

"Found something odd, Geoff," he said. "I was brushing away the dirt from this cluster, when I noticed that one of the eggs had a small piece of metal through its shell."

"Wait a minute," I said. "That's not possible—unless the site's been contaminated."

"Well, I don't think so. I mean, I was suspicious when I first found the thing, but look at it yourself."

I got down on my hands and knees in the dirt to examine the artifact more closely. The egg was reddish-purple in color, about nine inches across, and had been partially crushed in antiquity, leaving gray pieces of broken shell sticking out all around. Many dinosaur eggs just look like lumps of rock, particularly to civilians; this one, unusually, could have been identified almost immediately by anyone.

"Nice specimen," I said. "Rare to find them this good."

"Yeah, but…."

He showed me the other side of the thing. I had to scrunch around to see what he was looking at. Sticking right through one of the exposed pieces of fossilized eggshell was a slender piece of bright metal. It gave every appearance of being original to the site.

"Does it penetrate all the way through?" I asked.

"Haven't finished separating it from its bed. Give me a couple more hours, if I'm lucky."

But it was actually dinnertime before he brought me the complete artifact.

"Careful," he said, gingerly placing the heavy rock in my hand.

"I'll be damned."

A metal spike had penetrated the center of the egg from top to bottom.

"It's got to be a fake," I said, passing it back to him.

"Maybe, but I really don't think so."

"But if it isn't?"

"Yeah. *Yeah!*"

"Duke, no one will believe this." I shook my head.

"So, what are you going to do?"

"I'm going to keep my mouth shut and put it away, and so are you. You know what'll happen to our funding if we unveil this thing."

"OK."

And that was all he said.

I knew the world wasn't ready for this. If the stone was genuine, only two conclusions were possible: the dinosaurs (some of them, at least) had begun working metal in the years before their demise; or someone else had been taking potshots at them. Neither theory would have been acceptable to the worldwide community of paleontologists. It wouldn't make any difference what kind of evidence we presented. It just wouldn't fly, and Alver knew the truth of it as well as I.

"OK, boss," he said again, and went back to the dig.

Someday, I thought to myself, someday I'll have the metal analyzed and see what it reveals.

Someday.

But not today.

CHAPTER TWO
KEEP WATCHING THE SKIES

Then I felt like some watcher of the skies
When a new planet swims into his ken.
—John Keats

ALEX SMITH, 16 BI-FEBRUARY, MARS YEAR II
NOVATO, CALIFORNIA, PLANET EARTH

It was just a year ago that I finished my manuscript, *Keep Watching the Skies: My Story of the War of Two Worlds*. It was published in December on the second anniversary of the War, and I'm pleased to say that it's done surprisingly well, particularly considering the number of volumes about the Martian War that were released in the immediate aftermath of the conflict.

I wrote my book at least partially to gain support for a renewed effort on the part of our government, in concert with our allies around the world, to prepare for the next attack from Mars, an attack that I believe to be inevitable. Of course, my work stirred up reactions from all the usual "crazies," those folks who seem to find any excuse whatever for their wild imaginings and implausible schemes. One of these, I thought, was Dr. Geoffrey Alexander.

He first wrote to me shortly after the book appeared, saying that he had an artifact that he wanted me to examine. I didn't bother to reply. By then I was being snowed by "fan" mail, and had finally given up trying to answer it all. I still teach philosophy at the State U., and my life is now centered mostly on my family and my academic career. Mars (I hope) has finally been purged from my consciousness. Well, mostly.

I still have nightmares and I still wake up with cold sweats in the wee hours of the morning. I don't think that'll ever go away. And I still regret what happened to Reverend Lesley.

But I also have a daughter now, a precocious one-year-old who is constantly surprising her parents with her perceptiveness and intelligence and beauty; and her presence has irrevocably altered my life for the good.

Alexander didn't give up easily. He contacted my friend, Dr. Mindon Min, and convinced him of the reality of the thing; and Mindon set up a meeting between us three at Zee's, a funky little eatery in downtown Novato.

You need to understand something about Zee. He'd served in Iraq many years before. Something had gone wrong there— he'd seen too much or done too much or sniffed too much, no one really knew which—but when he returned to Northern California he bought a café called Crumbly's, and changed the name to Zee's Zippy Zone. The *décor* was as eclectic as Zee himself.

The walls were lined with what Mindon called "Old Shit," photos and implements and advertisements from the past, garnered from who knows where. Some of the larger doodads dangling from the ceiling swayed each time a patron entered or exited the place—or whenever we had an earthquake.

But it wasn't just the atmosphere that kept people coming back. Zee was a damned good cook, and he fixed something different every day. Even when he appeared to repeat a dish, there was something new or unusual about it, some twist that hadn't been there before. He didn't offer a menu as such: you either ate what he served you that day—or you didn't. I don't think Zee really cared one way or the other. Strangely, even the teens seemed to love the place, maybe because he told one of them once that he'd actually fried some bugs up (I never saw them!).

So Mindon set up the confab, and I reluctantly agreed to go along, just for my friend's sake, really. The events of the war had brought us even closer together than before, and he was one person (other than Becky) whom I didn't want to lose.

When I got there, I saw him sitting with Dr. Alexander over in our favorite corner.

"You're a hard man to get ahold of," the paleontologist said.

"I try to be," I said. "Don't really like publicity all that much."

"Then why write that book?"

"I felt that the world needed a wake-up call."

"So you don't think the Martian threat is over?"

"Nope."

"Neither do I, but my reasons are different from yours. You might say they're buried in the past. Take a look at this."

He reached into a knapsack and pulled out an ovoid object about nine inches in diameter, almost purple in hue, with flakes of gray-colored stone splattered all around the outside.

"It's the crushed egg of a duck-billed dinosaur, a hadrosaur," he said, "dating from the late Cretaceous period, or right near the end of the Age of Reptiles. Notice anything odd about it?"

He carefully laid the heavy stone in my palm.

"What're these prongs?" I pointed to several pieces of sharp metal protruding out of either side of the artifact.

"Well, that's the $24,000 question, isn't it? I thought at first it was a fake—we find them occasionally, even on the remote sites, seeded into otherwise pristine beds—but I've changed my mind. Problem was, I and the guy who discovered the thing couldn't make it public. We'd've been laughed right out of town. No one in the scientific community would have believed that it was genuine, not under any circumstance. Eventually, I had a sliver of the metal analyzed, but that too was something unique. No one could place it—at least until the Martian invasion.

"A couple of essays appeared in *Nature* this past year, providing the first detailed metallurgical analyses of the Martian machines. Now, here's the interesting thing: one of these profiles exactly matches the composition of the metal embedded in this sixty-five-million-year-old dinosaur egg."

"*Which one?*" I asked, suddenly very much interested indeed.

"A piece of a Martian spaceship," Alexander said. "They're exactly the same."

"But that means…."

"Yes," he said, smiling. "It means that the Martians were here sixty-five million years ago. It means that the asteroid that killed the dinosaurs wasn't an accident. It means that there was an earlier War of Two Worlds. And it means that we lost—big time! It means that all of the larger animals on Earth were killed as a result, slaughtered almost to the last one."

"Jeez," I said, "If they have that kind of technology…?"

"…Yeah, they could use it again," Mindon interjected, "and we're just sitting ducks, gents, one gigantic bull's-eye called Planet Earth."

"I'd like to have this verified myself, if that's possible," I said.

"Of course. That's why I brought it. You've been getting an awful lot of media play over your book, even now. People in the right places need to know about this. They *really* need to know right away."

He pulled out a folder and laid it on the table.

"This has all the documentation about the find, as described by me and Duke Alver, who was the one who actually stumbled on the thing. We were on a dig together in Montana a few years back. This one's given me a lot of sleepless nights on the Procrustean bed, let me tell you. I'm happy to share the burden."

"What about Duke?" I asked.

"Bought the farm couple of years ago."

Then Zee brought our lunches, and laid them before us. It was something made with cheese (more than one kind), pastrami, 'shrooms, spinach, onions, and a few other things. The odor was overwhelmingly pleasing.

The restaurateur stopped suddenly, and then examined the artifact with a very odd expression on his face.

"E-e-egg!" he finally managed to choke out.

"Yes it is, Zee," I said.

He shook his head: "D-don't l-let it ha-hatch!"
Then he walked away. We looked at each other.
"Let's eat," I finally said.
"Sufficient unto the day is the evil thereof," Mindon added.

CHAPTER THREE
FISH OUT OF WATER

Water, water, everywhere, nor any drop to drink.
—Samuel Taylor Coleridge

MINDON MIN, 21 BI-FEBRUARY, MARS YEAR II
NOVATO, CALIFORNIA, PLANET EARTH

After meeting Geoff and Alex the other day at Zee's, and seeing the evidence of Geoff's dinosaur egg, I didn't know what to think. Shit, paleontologists have been tossing around ideas about the Great Dino Demise for as long as I can remember. Of course, everything changed when Luis and Walter Álvarez discovered that iridium was present in abundance in the K-T Boundary, where it shouldn't have been.

K-T is a thin layer of fossilized clay demarcating the transition between the Cretaceous Period, the third and last act dominated by the dinosaurs, and the Tertiary Period, in which the mammals took over. No big animals of any kind survived the passage of that barrier. Iridium is a rare earth element relatively uncommon on Earth, but much more prevalent in meteorites. The Álvarezes (father and son) had postulated that a comet or asteroid roughly six miles in diameter hit the Earth circa sixty-five million BCE. An appropriately sized and dated crater was later discovered on the Yucatán Peninsula in México.

Q.E.D.

But if Geoff's find was real, then all bets were off. It meant the asteroid had possibly been nudged from its original orbit onto a collision course with Earth, and that the resulting nuclear winter had wiped out the dinos—and a good many other critters as well. But could the aliens actually have survived that long? It seemed a trifle improbable to me.

I put my eye back to the aperture of the 'scope, on the porch of my "Womb Tomb," as I called it—my retreat from civilization.

"Mindon, I'm back!"

That was Puff Santiago, my current S.O. Her real name was Hazel or Maude or some other godawful thing like Porfiria, but she preferred Puff. What could I say? We're all a little pseudonymous around here.

She'd run by Sargent's Pepper Pot to pick up some din-din. I particularly liked a dish called the Eye of Flame, a stew of meat and vegetables that was so heavily seasoned with pepper and ginger and chili that it would leave you gasping for mercy—and for more, more, more. Pam the Pulchritudinous Proprietress was gracious enough to accommodate any reasonable culinary request.

So I abandoned my heavenly observations of the sky to observe the heavenly measurements of someone else.

"You see it again?" La Puff asked.

She was remarkably easy on the eyes, with long auburn hair and a plump body and a wry smile that would just make your heart jump in your throat. I always felt better when she was there. Maybe this was the one who would actually lead me down the road to the Proposition Palace. Maybe she should.

"Nah," I said, "nothing."

Just a few months earlier, there'd been an opposition of Earth and Mars, the first since the Martian invasion. That's when the two planets reach their closest point to each other in their respective orbits. It happens once every twenty-six months between the red world and our blue one.

I'd been out there with all the rest of the amateur astronomers, night after night, looking for any signs of a new Martian invasion, but saw nothing—then!

But two days ago, just after my meeting with Alex, I noticed an isolated flash. It wasn't reported on any of the usual web or news sites or even on CNN. Truth be told, I wasn't even sure if what I'd seen was real, it happened so quickly. A little tinge of red, that's all it was. It could have been a reflection from a car's brakes or something. It hadn't been repeated.

"What do you think it was?" Puff asked, as we sat down to dinner.

"Don't know. The more I think about it, the less certain I am."

I heaped a ladle full of "Flame" onto a thick slice of the homemade organic wheat-berry bread that Pam had contributed to the package. One bite and I could already feel the endorphins hitting my bloodstream.

"Man, that's good!" I said.

Puff couldn't say anything at all.

"The problem is, it's too late in the season for the Martians to be launching a second invasion fleet. The planets are rapidly drifting apart. So if it was an alien ship, and it's not headed here, where's it going?"

She raised her fork.

"Maybe they've got other bases nearby. Maybe there's a Martian outpost in the Asteroid Belt."

"Maybe lots of things," I said, "but I don't like any of them. I hate this waiting. I hate wondering what they'll do next."

"What would you do about it if you had the chance?"

That's what I liked about Puff: she was never predictable.

"Me? Oh, I'd probably try communicating with them. What about you?" I asked.

She smiled sweetly while daintily popping a chili into her mouth.

"I'd bomb the bejesus out of them," she said.

CHAPTER FOUR
UP YOUR ASTEROID!

Streamed like a meteor to the troubled air.
—Thomas Gray

ALEX SMITH, 12 BI-JULY, MARS YEAR II
NOVATO, CALIFORNIA, PLANET EARTH

As usual, my wife was very supportive.

"Well, what the hell did you expect, Alex?" she asked. "You think they're just going to drop everything at your say-so and pour hundreds of billions of dollars into a space defense system? It's just not going to happen."

"But...."

"I don't care how convincing your evidence is, they'll just want to study it some more. I do love you, Alex, but sometimes you're the most impractical man on Planet Earth."

I knew she was right, of course, but that didn't make it any easier. The Bush III Administration had said that the Middle Eastern War had priority over any "possible" second invasion from Mars. After all, the Martians had been defeated, right? Man had proven his superiority once again. We were learning to adapt their technology, the experts said.

Balderdash! Man had been decisively squashed by the alien machines. The Martians had only died because of bacterial infection. Furthermore, we hadn't been able to make any of the Martian devices work; we couldn't replicate their bioengineering, hadn't even come close. We didn't understand any of it.

"They're going to come back," I said.

"You don't know why they invaded us in the first place." Becky waved her hands in frustration. "You don't know *squat* about them, really. Nobody does. They may return—or they may not.

"Anyway, I don't want to talk about it anymore. Mellie'll be up soon, and I want to read some more of my book before she is."

I raised an eyebrow.

She sighed heavily, and then very deliberately picked the volume up, displaying the garish cover to me: *The Martian Mystique: What It Means and Why We Should Be Worried!* by Madame Stavroula.

"Not her again," I groaned. "She's a charlatan, you know."

"She has some *very* interesting things to say about the aliens," Becky said. "Sure, some of it's hokum, and some of it's exaggerated; but she claims to have had visions of the Martian hives, and it rings true to me."

"And she's getting these, uh, visions from where? Come on, Becky, this is pretty rum stuff. I mean, hocus-pocus and all that. Hives? Like they're bugs or something?"

"She says, and I quote, 'The Martians are the surviving dominant life form of the Red Planet. When their world began to dry, when the waters finally receded for the last time, the Martians took their civilization underground, preserving those species that they needed to maintain themselves. In their hideaways they built their salt and fresh water cisterns and living spaces and gardens and laboratories, and for a billion years or more, they have worked to develop their culture, their defensive capabilities, and their art'."

"Art?" I just laughed and shook my head. "And what does our dear Madame S. have to say about the war?"

"She says they're not inherently an aggressive species, but they were attacked by another off-world race many millions of years ago, and nearly wiped out. They just barely managed to survive by finally destroying their enemy. This has made them paranoid about any perceived incursions on their own world. Our probes, Madame Stavroula says, were perceived as an attack on Mars, and so they responded in kind. The expedition they sent was intended as much to gather information as to measure the level of the threat we represented."

"That's why they killed millions of human beings?"

"They don't know anything about that. She says they never had any communication with their fleet after they made landfall. All they know is that the expedition never responded to their messages. Therefore, they assume that we killed them all, and that we have a greater technology than they do. Madame Stavroula says they will now take all appropriate measures to insure their safety."

"Well, at least she agrees that the aliens are still a threat," I said, laughing.

Then the phone rang. It was Min.

"Hey, man, turn on CNN right away!"

"What?"

"Right away, turn it on!"

"What is it, Alex?" Becky asked.

I grabbed the remote and clicked on the news.

"Reports are coming in," the newscaster said, "of a massive tsunami sweeping the coasts of Africa and South America."

"God, another earthquake," Becky said, "those poor people."

"No, man," Mindon yelled over the phone, "it's *not* an earthquake, it's the *Martians!*"

"What do you mean?"

"Remember the dino egg?" Mindon asked. "I'll bet you dollars to donuts they've lobbed one of those damned things at Earth."

"It's too soon, Mindon," I said. "The last opposition was months ago, and the two planets have been moving away from each other ever since. Couldn't be an asteroid."

"Think, man! It takes a long time to move something like a meteor around, even if it already crosses Mars's and Earth's

orbits. Too much mass. It'd take years to nudge it just right, depending on what kind of engine you had and how close the thing would get to Earth naturally. This wasn't started months ago. They probably got it moving right after the war. And this was just a small rock."

The news on the TV was more serious now.

"According to Henry Newbolt in our London office, all communication with the Falkland Islands has been lost. The island of Aladore has been obliterated from the map. Survivors are reporting one-hundred-foot waves striking some of the major coastal cities of South America.

"And this just in! We have reports of a massive explosion, maybe an atom bomb, in the southern Atlantic Ocean."

"It was a meteor, I tell you." Then I hung up.

Eventually, Mindon and Puff came over, and we sat there all through the rest of the afternoon and early evening glued to the TV set, watching the damage and casualty reports continue to mount. No one knew what'd caused the event. Pictures began to come in of the devastated cities.

"It's the invasion all over again," I said. "I keep thinking about the War of Two Worlds."

The phone rang. Becky answered it, and then looked at me strangely, holding the instrument in her right hand.

"It's someone from the National Security Council," she said. "They want to talk to *you*, Alex."

CHAPTER FIVE
THE SHIP THAT SAILED TO MARS

An eye like Mars, to threaten and command.
—William Shakespeare

ALEX SMITH, 15 BI-MARCH, MARS YEAR VII
U.S.S. ARMAGEDDON, IN ORBIT AROUND PLANET EARTH

"'Beware the Ides of March!'" I said, pulling myself into the Colonel's office.

I'd come aboard just a week earlier, one of a group of advisers assigned to the multinational expedition that was currently being mounted against the Red Planet. I was still trying to get used to the absence of gravity, although the officer "sitting" before me certainly made up for it. He was actually roped into a kind of hanging chair.

"And I suppose 'All of Gaul is divided into three parts'." Timlett replied, quoting the ancient military genius, Gaius Julius Cæsar.

He was a middle-sized man with a wiry physique and close-cropped hair; like Cassius, he had that "lean and hungry look."

I chuckled.

"So you know some history after all," I said.

"Well, I did read the great military minds back in school, not that any of them has really prepared me for what we're about to face here."

"I don't think that anything would, except surviving the

damned war. And if we don't get the job done, and soon, the Martians will continue pounding poor Earth back into the Stone Age."

"We're still on target, Doctor," he said. "We'll make our launch date two weeks hence. If some of the supply vessels aren't ready, we'll go without them. We have to.

"Now, do you have something specific in mind, or can I get back to work?"

"I, uh, I would most respectfully request once again that you leave my wife and daughter on Earth, sir. This is no place for civilians."

"Well, Doctor Smith, ordinarily I would be the first to agree with you," he said, "but I have no choice in the matter. My orders are explicit. The so-called 'Sensitives' are here because they may offer the only hope we have of communicating with the aliens—or of understanding their motives. I'm sorry your womenfolk are among them, truly I am.

"Me personally, I don't really believe in all this crap, and I certainly don't like the idea of having to watch over and feed some additional mouths that I think will contribute very little to our expedition. But, as I said...."

"You have your orders."

"Yes, sir, I do, and I would remind you that although you're also a civilian, you still come under my direct authority as Captain of this vessel. Now, is there anything else?"

"There is."

I floated over to the little porthole, one of the few privileges of rank accorded the officer. I never tired of looking down at the blue-green vistas sliding below us. From this height you would never guess what Earth had gone through these past dozen years. Over a hundred million men, women, and children dead or injured, many more millions displaced, dozens of cities completely wiped from memory, major damage to shipping and industry—the toll went on and on and on.

The Martian bombardment had continued, year after year, even when we'd developed the first of our planetary defensive systems and created the United States Space Force. There were always a few rocks that slipped through the net, despite our best efforts. We had to stop them at the source. We had to conquer or destroy Mars any way possible, even at the cost of our own lives. It was us or them, and I was damn well determined that it would be us that walked away from the fight.

While I was contemplating my next question, the Colonel's com phone buzzed.

"Yes," he said.

"Col. Morris, sir," the orderly said, "line two."

"Put him through."

"Beau!" came the voice of the *Thunderbolt*'s captain.

"What's up, Bill?"

"We need to borrow one of your engineers again."

One of the very few pieces of Martian technology that our scientists had successfully adapted for our own use was the ion drive from the alien spaceships, but it was a tricky piece of work, requiring constant readjustment.

"Sure," he said. "I'll send him over through the pipeline"—both ships were connected via a giant umbilical cord with the space dock—"Anything else we can do for you?"

"Throw in a how-to manual, and I'll feel a whole lot better. I just keep wondering if we're going to be able to launch on schedule."

"The main fleet is pretty much ready," Timlett said, "although we still have some supplies we're waiting for; but the other ships are lagging behind. They're concentrating on finishing the main armada first. I talked with Fritz yesterday, and he says that we're a 'go' on April the First no matter what else is ready. If necessary, they'll send the rest of the boats on later."

"How far can they stretch the window?"

"A month, maybe two; anything beyond that, and we start running into fuel problems with the shuttles, not to mention delivery issues at the other end. I think they'll keep launching them anyway, trusting that most of the pods will get through sooner or later. Even later is better than never."

"True," Morris said. "I trust the lovely ladies are keeping you pleasantly occupied."

"Shit," Timlett muttered, looking over his shoulder at me. "The eggheads are bad enough, but the women...."

"Be happy with what you've got, my friend. They started bringing up the Marines and Special Ops forces yesterday, together with the regular Army boys. Today one of them rigged a zero-G toilet so the next person who used it got stuck to the damned thing. We had to dismantle the seat to get the poor slob loose."

Timlett started laughing.

"What did you do to him?"

"I thought about sending him downside, but that was probably what he was looking for in the first place. His file indicates that he was included on this mission because of his extensive experience with the Martians during the War. So I just took one of his stripes instead. Oh, yeah, I'm sending him over to you as staff liaison."

"Oh, thanks a whole lot."

"I have another little fly I'd like to buzz your way too. Our new Chaplain, the Very Reverend Captain Lesley, is a royal pain in the butt. She keeps complaining about the lack of facilities and the cramped working conditions and just about everything else. I have to remind her each and every time that this is a military vessel. I think she'd fit right in with your little group of ladies."

I perked up immediately on hearing the minister's name. This couldn't be the same person, could it? The Lesley I knew had been killed in the War, harvested by the Martians during my two-week imprisonment in the demolished house in Marin County.

"Uh, don't think so, Bill. I've already got enough on my plate. You can barter with God, if you want."

"Gee, Beau, I'm so blessed."

I could hear another buzzing somewhere off in the distance.

"Got to sign off," the Captain of the *Thunderbolt* said. "Keep on flying, partner!"

"You too, Bill. Take care of yourself."

The two colonels were both good men from what I'd seen. I wasn't as sure of Major General Fritz Burgess, Commander of the expedition: I just didn't know him personally, had only met him once, in fact, at a planning session at the Pentagon. He had the reputation of being a real hard ass, but given the nature of our mission, perhaps that was just as well. Still, I was glad that the designated flagship vessel and primary military transport of the fleet was the *Thunderbolt* and not the *Armageddon*.

"What else, Smith?" came the query, waking me out of my reverie. "I do have a few other things on my plate."

I cleared my throat.

"Do you know anything about Reverend Lesley? I met somebody by that name during the War."

"No, sir, but you can access the public portions of her file through the ship's library database. The ship rosters can be reviewed by anyone."

"Thanks, I didn't know that," I said. "On another matter, I've been selected by my colleagues to represent their interests on this mission. They're concerned about the absence of any formal mechanism by which they can both receive intelligence about the Martians and provide feedback to you and your colleagues. I realize that you have no choice about including us on this trip, but I do think you could take some better advantage of our cumulated experience and knowledge."

"You do, huh?" the Colonel said. "Look, Doctor, I'm trying to get this boat launched on time. That's all I'm interested in right now. Once we actually get going we'll have more leisure in which to discuss what happens when we finally reach Mars.

"All of you should understand at least this much, however: I and my superior officers have the ultimate decision-making authority on this mission. Yes, I will attempt to consult with you people whenever it seems appropriate. Yes, I may even listen to you on occasion. Right now, though, we have a job to do. I can't let anything else interfere with that. Any other questions, comments, or issues, *Doctor*?"

I shook my head "no."

"Then you're dismissed," he said, and went back to his screen, using his wand to approve the various dispositions pending before him.

I was left to pull myself through the door hole. The guard stationed in the corridor outside didn't even bother to salute.

CHAPTER SIX
CROSSING THE RIVER

Let us cross over the river, and rest under the trees.
—Stonewall Jackson

ALEX SMITH, 1 BI-APRIL, MARS YEAR VII
U.S.S. ARMAGEDDON, IN ORBIT AROUND PLANET EARTH

The day had at last arrived. Everything that I'd worked for during the previous years was finally coming to fruition. We were going to launch the main assault fleet in just over an hour.

This wasn't the first manned journey to Mars, of course. During the most recent pair of oppositions between Earth and the Red Planet, we'd sent several small groups of probes and weapon ships and observation platforms there, just to learn what we could expect in response. All of the brave men and women on Expedition I had died very quickly in Bi-April of Year Five. Half of those on Expedition II had perished within months of their arrival in Bi-June of Six, and another half of the survivors had perished in the interim; but the remaining fifty or so veterans were waiting for us at their bases on the Martian moons of Phobos and Deimos.

Phobos is the larger of the satellites, and since it orbits relatively close to the planet (about 5,600 miles from its surface), it provided our forces with a fairly safe and secure hideaway once they managed to dig in. A small automated Martian observation station there was destroyed by our sappers. We also established a second, smaller base on Deimos, the outer moon. Both camps had extensive laser and missile defensive and offensive systems. Curiously, the aliens had made no attempt to assault either facility. Also, neither base had reported any additional or unusual activity on the surface of Mars in response to the construction of our fleet.

What these two previous raids had also established, however, was the type and scale of weaponry we would have to face once we arrived at the Red Planet.

The first of these was a long-range adaptation of the Martian sting-ray (essentially a souped-up laser); this development had been predicted by the engineers who had salvaged and analyzed these weapons from the great striding tripods abandoned by the aliens during the War of Two Worlds. We'd already developed our own versions of these systems, together with several possible defensive mechanisms and reflective metal shields. They weren't regarded as a major military threat.

The second weapon employed by the Martians was a kind of cosmic pea-shooter. The atmosphere and gravity on the Red Planet are both sufficiently slight that small projectiles can actually be fired from the surface without too much expenditure of energy. In essence, the aliens were using giant cannon to pepper our spacecraft and bases with fast-moving rocks of varying sizes. Later, they employed a variation of this by shooting small cluster-bombs at our ships. These would explode before actually hitting anything, scattering dozens or hundreds of fast-moving metal or stone pellets at their targets. The result was deadly.

We were eventually able to build our own versions of these giant sling-shots on Phobos Base, and thereafter we were able to respond in kind to any alien attacks; by Year Seven we'd put all of the known launching sites on Mars out of commission.

During those initial expeditions, our forces reported seeing very few Martian spaceships as such. I suspect that these were just too valuable as primary assets to be wasted in wanton and risky attacks on our fleets.

We still didn't know for sure where the aliens were modifying the meteor orbits to allow them to hit the Earth. Mindon believed that the Martians had one or more bases out in the Asteroid Belt, including the minor planet Ceres, and were installing their ion engines on selected rocks that crossed the Earth's orbit. Even so, it would take many years in some instances to generate enough of an aberration in the paths of these asteroids to make them a danger to our planet.

We knew for certain of about a dozen rocks that had been lobbed in our direction, beginning with that first strike in Year Two. Several had been near misses; several others had been detected by our long-range radar, and had either been nudged sufficiently to remove them from the danger list or had been split into a number of pieces by well-placed nuclear bombs. Half a dozen meteorites, however, had actually struck Earth dead center, causing horrendous damage to our ecology and our economy.

We practically had to mortgage the planet to mount the response that was now being launched. Every nation in the world had contributed, even third-world countries. No one was left out. The cost had already reached into the many trillions of dollars. The damage caused by the Martian pounding of Earth had added trillions more. The world would forever be a different place because of the War of Two Worlds.

"Daddy," my twelve-year-old daughter Mellie exclaimed, "look!"

She pointed to the viewscreen. We were all locked in our small cabins for the departure, on the orders of General Burgess, and were watching the proceedings through the official ship communications channel. I wondered if Mindon was enjoying "Duck Dodgers" on the Cartoon Network.

The nearby Bellerophon Orbital Defense Station was hosting the major world leaders, including the Presidents of the United States, Russia, China, the European Community, La Comunidad Latina, India, the Organization of African States, and the al-Jihadi Arab Coalition, plus the Secretary General of the United Nations, among others.

Displayed on the screen were the large space docks containing the *Armageddon*, the *Thunderbolt*, the *T-Rex*, the *Phoenix*, the *Uhuru*, the *Yarost'*, the *Fléau*, the *Hasta*, the *Huracán*, the *Van Dine*, and the *Annihilation*. Surrounding these were some 200 points of light representing the attack, transport, and support vessels of the fleet.

We were going to Mars to stay.

"It's beautiful, Daddy!" Mellie said.

Then President Bush's face appeared, the former Governor of California close by her side.

"We inaugurate this expedition to save all mankind," she intoned. "May you go with God's good grace and all of our blessings. The hopes and future of the world journey with you."

The ex-Governor then stepped forward, holding a document in his right hand where everyone could see.

"General Fleming Thomas Burgess: in accordance with the authority granted to me by the United Nations and the United States of America, you are hereby requested and required to assume command of Mars Expedition III, and to proceed at flank speed to the Red Planet, where you will undertake any and all steps necessary to defeat the enemy and to secure his territory.

"Let's go kick some Martian butt!" the politician then shouted, to the cheers of the official delegation and the watching billions around the globe.

General Burgess virtually received a copy of the proffered proclamation.

"On behalf of the men and women of Expedition III, I accept this sacred charge," he said. "Operation Crimson Storm has now commenced. We will defeat the Martians or die trying, sir."

Then he saluted from his station on the command deck of the *Thunderbolt*. I wasn't sure that an either-or proposition was entirely suitable to the occasion.

Half an hour later the grand armada began to move, very slowly at first, but gradually, oh so gradually gathering speed as the ships' ion engines came on line. They would continue to accelerate until the mid-point of their journey, and then decelerate all the rest of the way to the Red Planet.

Only one thing marred the departure: the *H.M.S. Wells* just sputtered a bit and sat dead in the water, so to speak. It would join the rest of the fleet as soon as they could find a Scottish engineer to clean out the pipes.

They let us out of our cages an hour after departure. I guess they figured that anything that could have gone wrong would already have happened by then.

The acceleration was minor enough that it had no real effect on our senses: the ship still felt like a zero-G environment. You either got used to it or you didn't. I knew of one poor slob who spent the entire blasted trip vomiting out his insides, and was so happy finally to land on Mars that he completely forgot his basic training, and accidentally killed himself by failing to secure his helmet adequately. Oh, well, these things happen.

All in all, though, I found the occasion very positive and gratifying. To quote one of my dippier colleagues, we took a partridge from a lemon tree and shook some lemonade out of it. We were finally taking action against the aliens! I had no doubt whatever that we'd prevail.

Sometimes, though, winning a war isn't everything.

Sometimes it doesn't amount to very much at all.

CHAPTER SEVEN
ON THE THRESHOLD

The inevitability of gradualness.
—Lord Passfield & Beatrice Webb

ALEX SMITH, 26 BI-MAY, MARS YEAR VII
U.S.S. ARMAGEDDON, IN TRANSIT FROM EARTH TO MARS

I think Becky was secretly pleased to have been included on the expedition, although I know she wasn't too happy about our daughter being there. I'd tried to get both of them removed from the ship before our departure, of course, but without any success.

I believe that it was President Bush who'd had the last word on the subject. She'd been influenced by that thrice-damned charlatan, Madame Stavroula, to add the psychics to our group of advisers, over the strenuous objections of both the scientific and military communities.

"Maybe it means nothing," she said, "and maybe they will add nothing, but right now they seem to have more answers than any of the rest of you."

"With all respect, Ma'am," General Burgess had said, "their so-called answers are unverifiable speculations, based on nothing tangible that I or anyone else can discern. This woman means well, I'm sure, but she and her little group of fortune tellers will consume a great deal of our limited supplies of food and water while we're trying to determine the veracity of their speculations."

But the real "Madame" got her way, as usual, and so the Sensitives were included among the ship's company. Even the ex-Governor had to defer to her on such occasions, despite his public blustering.

Mostly, though, I saw very little of them. The women kept largely to themselves. I knew from Becky, their elected representative on the Expedition Advisory Council, that their dreams and visions continued to intensify as we progressed further in our journey through space. Why only certain female members of the species had been affected in this way was the subject of much speculation by psychologists, including Dr. Emil Kürnig, a member of my own group on the expedition.

"Ve see dat the intuitive nature of the Ayesha pershona now ish coming to the foreground," he would mumble, "und ve undershtand how it is dat dish ting, it ish accompolished."

Frankly, I hadn't a clue as to what he was talking about, but he was like that sometimes. He was much more personable when drinking beer, which of course was forbidden on the ship, along with anything else of an alcoholic nature (although I believe that Mindon had somehow smuggled a flask of whiskey on board).

There were also a few children present, all of them over the age of six, and all offspring of other Sensitives; and of course my daughter Mélusine was among them. They seemed to adapt to ship life much more quickly than any of the rest of us.

Mellie would swoop down the corridors of Deck Three, our living quarters, using the hand-holds to swing like Tarzan's mate up and down the length of the vessel. I had to caution her several times after a couple of near collisions with adults.

A few days later I was paged on the com system to report to the Infirmary, where my daughter was being treated. Becky was already there when I arrived, breathless from having swung myself nearly the length of the ship.

"What happened?" I asked my wife.

I could barely see Mellie strapped to an examination table in the other room, several bloody cloths hanging in the air next to her.

Becky pulled me away from the door hole.

"She started bleeding a few hours ago," she whispered in my ear.

"Is it serious?" I asked.

My heart was pounding. This confirmed all of the fears that I'd had about bringing the women and children on this voyage.

"Menarche usually responds fairly well to treatment," she said smugly.

"Menarche? What kind of disease is that?"

"Her first period, Alex," Becky said.

"But, but, she's only twelve years old."

"It happens. Now, I suggest you go back to your pontificating and let me deal with this. I have a little more experience with these things, I think."

So I did.

That afternoon I was due at a meeting of Expedition III's Advisory Council. The issue of accountability and chain of command was coming to a head just after the midpoint on our journey. Burgess had created the group from the different constituencies represented in the fleet, including several of the military units. We were able to meet through videoconferencing in the various rooms established for that purpose on each major vessel. I represented the Thinkers, while my wife stood in for the Psychics, Jorys Johns for the Journalists, and Mindon Min for the Scientists, among others.

But Burgess continued to insist on the paramount role of the High Command, which he headed.

"Ladies and gentlemen," he finally said, after a particularly nasty and bruising meeting, "I'm afraid I'm going to have to insist on this particular point. I have the ultimate authority and responsibility for the safety of the men and women of the fleet, and for the success of our mission. I've given you my word that I'll listen to whatever you have to say. In the end, though, my decisions will be final. I have my orders, and ultimately your presence here makes you subject to those orders. Now, I think we've talked enough for one session."

Afterwards, I met with my own little group.

"Who the fucking hell does he think he is?" Anton Chernov, a Russian-American artist, asked.

"The Commander-in-Chief," I said.

"The overbearing son of a bitch!" came the response.

"He's got a point, though," Johns said. "On the battlefield, only one person can be in charge; otherwise, you've lost the war before it's even begun."

"Each of us is an expert in his own field," I said, "and the same is true of the members of the other groups. All of us have connections and constituencies back on Earth, and we've been guaranteed access to communications facilities even after we arrive on Mars. If there's information to be gathered or conclusions to be drawn, we'll find them."

"But how do we know they'll even listen?" Chernov asked. "I don't trust these military types, Alex; I don't trust them at all. They want easy solutions to everything. The universe is a complex place, my friends. If it was easy to defeat the aliens, we would have done so years ago."

"Maybe we did," I said.

"I don't believe that either," Chernov said. "I think the Martians still have a few surprises waiting for us out there. Bah!"

Then our meeting broke up. I got together that evening with Mindon and Geoff Alexander, the paleontologist, who'd somehow been added to the expedition at the last moment, by whom or for what purpose I had no idea (he didn't know himself).

"My people aren't happy," I said.

"Mine neither, man," Mindon said, "but what can you do? I have a tendency to believe that things work out pretty much as they're supposed to—even if you don't personally like the outcome."

"Yeah," I said, "but a bad outcome in this case could be the end of us all, not to mention our families and colleagues back on Earth."

"You know," Alexander said, "when I stumbled on that blasted dino egg back in '95, I felt like that damn metal spike was sticking right through the middle of me. I had a pretty good idea what it meant, even back then. But I was a lot younger in those days.

"I still go out on digs, but I don't believe any longer that I can find all the answers buried in the Montana rock fields. Maybe we'll discover a few more answers on Mars. Maybe we shouldn't allow ourselves to be trapped too soon by our own fossilized thinking."

"I've spent so much time speculating about the Martians and their motives," I said, "that I don't know what's true anymore and what isn't."

"Well," Mindon said, "I can think of a few things that remain true: 1) the aliens will be waiting for us whenever we get there; and 2) I'm really tired and need to get to bed—or at least what amounts to bed with those stupid hammock thingies."

We all laughed. Each of us had had problems getting ourselves entangled in the middle of the night in the blasted netting, which seemed to be designed with monkeys in mind, not human beings. I'd banged my head a couple of times on what passed for the ceiling in our small quarters.

Later that night, I talked with Becky as we were quite literally hanging off the wall together.

"What do your people think about all this?" I asked her quietly.

"Madame Stavroula believes that the answers are there for us to find, if we can open our hearts and minds to the possibilities."

"But what does she *really* think will happen?"

There was a long silence.

"She hasn't told me much, Alex," Becky finally said softly. "She won't tell me. I have the impression, and it's only that, that what she's envisioning isn't very promising. I think she's just afraid, and I'm not sure whether she's more afraid of the aliens or of our own people. Whenever I talk to her, she seems distracted somehow. I've never seen her like that before."

"I have," I said without thinking.

"What?"

"Hey, can you two please go to sleep?" my dear daughter hissed from the other side of the room. "I'm trying to get some rest over here. It's bad enough when you do that stuff of yours."

"Stuff?" I whispered in Becky's ear.

"You know, like this," she said, poking me.

"Oh," I said, squirming. "That! I'd almost forgotten."

"Poleeeze!" Mellie said. "I'm covering my ears now."

I didn't worry about Mars for quite some time. It's amazing what zero-G can do for your libido.

But before morning bells shook the ship from its slumber, I had the strangest dream.

It was dark. I was floating in a pool of sea water. I could taste the salt spray, and could hear the slight sloshing noise of the small waves as they tiptoed past me. The red weed caressed the underside of my body, tickling me and almost making me giggle. The growth swirled about as if it were animate. Then something grabbed my penis and pulled me down beneath the surface of the pool. I started gasping for air and blowing bubbles in my desperate attempt to get loose.

That's when I came to the surface again.

"Alex, what's wrong?" Becky asked, putting her arms around me.

I struggled for a moment to get free, still touched by the fronds of my imagination.

"What's the matter?"

"The weed," I managed to gasp. "It's Mars, Becky. It's reaching out for me."

She held me close until I stopped shuddering. I felt like I'd been violated.

"Now you know how I feel sometimes," she said.

CHAPTER EIGHT
DREAM STORY

Dreaming dreams no mortal ever dared to dream before.
—Edgar Allan Poe

ALEX SMITH, 3 BI-JULY, MARS YEAR VII
U.S.S. ARMAGEDDON, IN TRANSIT FROM EARTH TO MARS

But I wasn't the only one who had trouble sleeping during those long days of voyaging through the æther. The ladies were being increasingly bothered, almost on a daily basis, by visions, nightmares, even waking dreams of the Martian homeworld. A few of the male members of the expedition seemed to be headed in the same direction. The Advisory Council was charged with finding the commonality between these disparate groups, but other than the fact that all of the affected men seemed to have had some direct contact with the invaders more than a dozen years earlier, nothing else was obvious.

I left a message with Dr. Jarmann back on Earth. The xenobiologist had been invited to join the expedition, but had declined for personal reasons, being now rather elderly and not wanting to leave his Bavarian Mountain Retreat on the Zugspitze.

He spoke no English, and my German was insufficient to conduct a conversation, so we had to work back and forth through the translation programs available on the Interlink.

"Herr Doktor Smith," he said, when we finally made contact.

"Herr Doktor Jarmann," I said, explaining to him the reason

for my call.

"This is very interesting," the old scientist said. "As you know, we have been trying to sequence the DNA of the Martians and their plants, but it has taken us a very long time to get any results that are actually usable. The alien genome is extraordinarily different from ours, particularly since they reproduce asexually. This is true, by the way, of both the plant and animal life on Mars.

"What we have discovered, my young friend, is that there are surprising underlying similarities between all of the Martian life forms. The plants appear to share some of their genetic structures with the animate creatures of Mars, and vice versa. We do not know yet whether this is because they have been deliberately bred that way by the Martians, or whether this occurred naturally over a long period of time.

"We suspect that all of the Martian creatures live together symbiotically, that they each require something of the others to continue to survive and prosper. This would lead us naturally to the conclusion that the Martian intelligences actually died, not of infection by the Earthly microbes, as had been previously supposed (and which we had personally already discounted, since the Martians varied so widely in their physiology from any Earthly species); but through a failure to obtain some essential nutrient or ingredient necessary to their continued existence. Perhaps it was the inability of the Martian flora to establish themselves permanently on Earth that led to the demise of their masters."

"I find all this intriguing, of course," I said, "but what does it have to do with our present situation?"

"Ah," he replied, after the usual pause in communication caused by the huge distance the message had to travel from Earth to the *Armageddon*. "Do you know of any individuals who have been affected by this disease which we might have called the *Traumnovelle*?"

He employed here the title of an Arthur Schnitzler tale; it meant something like "Dream Story."

"Well, I've been having nightmares myself," I said, "and they've been getting steadily worse as we approach ever closer to Mars."

"*Ach*, this is what we might have expected," Jarmann said. "And you had some contact with the Martians in Upper California, no?"

I explained my brief history to him.

"This is not exactly what we meant by this interrogatory," he said. "What we really want to know is whether or not you actually touched a living Martian."

To the best of my knowledge, I hadn't. The tentacle of one of the handling-machines had brushed the heel of my foot (which was encased within its shoe), just briefly, during those terrible weeks I was trapped in the ruined house in Marin County, but I hadn't actually felt one of the buggers, and I told him so.

"What about the red weed or the other Martian growths?" he asked.

"The weed was everywhere," I said. "You couldn't move around without encountering the stuff. I stepped over and through big patches of it, I moved it out of the way with my hands, I even cut some pieces of the weed and ate it, I was so hungry."

"*Ach*," he said again. "Ahhhh! Well, there we have it, you see. You ingested some of the plant, and it has become part of you, my dear friend. Martian life is very adaptable, or so we have found. Even here on Earth, we have now discovered that the weed and its cousins did not totally disappear from our fields and streams, as we had first thought. In places it has now actually come back, never as much as before, but it has such an amazing capacity for survival. What an interesting species it is!"

"But you said yourself that Martian DNA is very different from ours," I noted.

"So we did," he said, "and this is true, my dear Doctor. Nonetheless, we suspect that the Martian genome is capable of adapting itself to an almost infinite variety of homes and environments, including other organic structures. Of course, some of my colleagues would disagree with this theory, and actually proving it will take many more years of research. Also, if such a transmission takes place, how much contact is actually required; and does the transmission proceed in both directions? All of these are very, very fascinating questions.

"We have ourselves eaten the red weed and pieces of the other Martian plants. We can fix them in a salad with a few fava beans, spinach, onions, pepper, chili, and olive oil, and they are, as you say, quite, quite delicious. They also mix well within an olio of lentil beans, well roasted pork, onions, cilantro, a sprinkling of havarti cheese, and black pepper. We have not yet perceived any of the dreams that you described, although we occasionally suffer from the gas and the indigestion."

He belched quite noticeably.

"Uh, thank you, Doktor," I said, and terminated the connection.

Later that day, I spotted my friend Mindon in the gym, and reported on my conversation with Jarmann. Min was working hard on a stationary cycle, where he had to strap himself into place to generate any tension. We had all been urged to do an hour's worth of exercise daily to avoid deterioration of our muscles; some of us did better at this than others.

"I thought you looked kind of red-faced these past few days," he stated, chuckling, his legs pumping furiously.

"Right," I said. "But what do you think? Is some kind of cross-transmission of genetic material actually possible between species?"

"I'm really the wrong person to ask," he replied. "You'd do better running that one by Zee."

"I would if I could," I said, laughing a little.

Zee was in no shape to answer much of anything these days.

"Well, Alex, you can," Mindon said. "I saw him just the other day."

"You're kidding me!"

"Swear to God. He served in the Guard, you know. They

called him up again when this expedition was being put together."

"But they couldn't," I said. "He's, he's, well, you know."

"He works down in Hydroponics. Helps fix some of the fresh veggies we've been having, I understand."

Eating salad in a zero-G environment was always a challenge, but having the newly-grown greens available was well worth the effort.

"It's like Old Home Week up here," I said. "All of the people that I knew during the War keep reappearing suddenly. I heard the other day that Reverend Lesley's still alive. She's apparently serving on the flagship."

"Really? I always thought she might be an interesting one to meet, from what you told me."

"You're certainly welcome to her. She's almost as bad as that blasted fortune teller, Madame Stavroula, who keeps turning up in my life like a bad Penelope."

Mindon stopped his pumping for a moment, and gazed at me very intently.

"You know, actually, Alex, I've run into her recently," he said. "She's not half bad. 'Stavroula's just a stage name, you know."

"Well, I could have guessed that one."

"Yeah, but her real name, oddly enough, is Nomsah."

"Nomsah." I ran it over my tongue. "You know, Min, that one sounds very familiar somehow."

"She says that her father was Greek and one of her grand-mothers or someone way-back-when was African, deriving originally from a mixed bloodline somewhere on Providence Island, wherever that is. Anyway, they had this tradition on both sides of her family of what she calls 'cheiromanteia' or something like that. The women were frequently 'moiraia gynaika,' which can apparently be interpreted in a number of different ways."

"Hey, I met her!" I suddenly clapped my hands and nearly lost my balance as a result. "Twice! The first time was in her guise as a palm reader, several years before the War, and the second time was during the conflict, when we were both stuck one night in a hotel on Nob Hill. She looked and acted completely different. I just never made the connection before. Amazing!"

"She has that ability to morph herself into whatever anyone wants to see," Mindon said.

Suddenly an alarm sounded.

"The ship is under attack! This is not a drill! Remain where you are and secure yourselves immediately! All airtight doors will automatically close in ten seconds."

The entrance porthole to the gym suddenly slid shut with a loud bang and a click.

"Now what?" I asked. "Another exercise?"

Night and day for weeks now, Colonel Timlett had been running the vessel through its paces. Even without the dreams, I wouldn't have gotten much sleep, I think.

"I don't think so," Mindon said, dismounting and pulling himself over to a chair, where he strapped himself in. The vessel suddenly began to rumble with a distant but distinct thudding.

"Those sound like our laser cannons to me."

"Cripes," I said, pulling myself across the room and also securing myself to one of the exercise chairs.

The *Armageddon* shuddered once with a deep-set trembling that signaled an impact somewhere on its massive frame.

"A hit!" Mindon said.

There were two more quivers that we could register before the "All Clear" signal was given.

I immediately headed for my cabin, where I found Becky and Mellie safe and secure, watching the ship's communications channel.

"What are they saying?" I asked.

"Somehow they lobbed a rock several hundred feet in diameter at the fleet," she replied, "and we didn't detect it until now. One of our 'Interference Runners' hit it squarely and blew it to bits, the remnants peppering the *Armageddon* and several other ships. The *Rapace* was badly damaged; they say it'll have to be stripped and abandoned. They lost at least half their crew through massive depressurization."

"What about us?"

"We're OK, all of us," she said, turning around and smiling at me. She had one arm around Mellie's waist, holding her in place. "The ship's OK and we're OK, Alex."

CHAPTER NINE
FAREWELL, EARTH'S BLISS

Chance favors only the mind that's prepared.
—Louis Pasteur

ALEX SMITH, 31 BI-JULY, MARS YEAR VII
U.S.S. ARMAGEDDON, IN ORBIT AROUND PLANET MARS

Different elements of the main fleet actually arrived on Mars station in various stages, as had previously been planned. Some of the ships had augmented their ion drives with chemical or nuclear rockets, or had lighter payloads, deliberately to allow them to dock earlier than the huge transport vessels.

Among these were the great circular Warstations, heavily armored craft with thick hull plating and numerous offensive weapons; these were designed to be parked permanently over the planet in stationary orbit, spaced out evenly around the globe. They would provide cover for the arrival of our main fleet, and also take an integral part in the ongoing military operations that would commence soon thereafter. In theory, at least, the entire surface of Mars could be scanned simultaneously from the heavens once the stations were deployed.

A second group of advance ships consisted of the Interference Runners, which had been sent out in front of the fleet to defend it from just such an attack as had occurred recently. These unmanned craft were filled with explosives, and were intended to ram and blow up anything physical that the Martians might heave our way. Once they reached Mars proper, they would be used to bombard selective targets on the surface, and thus gradually be used up.

Also deployed in advance of the fleet were a few strange-looking cylinders that would eventually be unfolded at one end, opening up faces that looked almost like giant metallic umbrellas. The surfaces on the outside of these ships were so polished that they reflected back to their source nearly 100% of all the visible light waves they received. This was one major defense against the amplified Martian sting-rays, enough, we hoped, to allow the Warstations to find and target the surface emplacements generating the rays before they could do any actual damage to our ships.

The fleet had to be deployed in a certain sequence in order to be effective. We intended to use the Martian moons to shadow and protect many of our initial operations, while the Warstations were still being maneuvered into their final orbital positions.

The first ships arrived at Mars on July the Eleventh, and were immediately moved into their "watch-and-defend" positions over the planet. The most vulnerable period for the Warstations was the initial week, as they were jockeyed into their permanent geosynchronous orbits. Cover was partially provided by the Martian moons, but these transited so quickly across the sky (Phobos circled the Red Planet in just seven hours) that their ability to target any particular site on the planet was often severely limited. Two of the stations, the *Buenos Aires* and the *Miami,* were destroyed in the first few days, but these losses had been anticipated, and we had more than enough surplus coverage to spare.

The core of the fleet, which included the *Armageddon* and the other big transports, attained high Mars orbit on the last day of July. We were using the umbrella ships to shadow Phobos from attacks by the sting-rays, while the *Thunderbolt* was carefully maneuvered into position in the shadow of the inner Martian moon. Then General Burgess officially moved his seat of command to Phobos Base, and the troops and supplies were quickly offloaded from the vessel into the caves and structures that had been prepared for them over the past two years by the advance scouting party from Expedition II.

The Martians tried to penetrate our orbital defensive wall on several occasions, but in each case one of the Interference Runners was directed onto the site of the Martian surface emplacement, which was utterly destroyed in the ensuing explosion. Resistance there gradually diminished as the debarkation of the fleet continued.

The *Armageddon* was next in line. *Thunderbolt* was gradually moved into higher orbit, preparatory to starting on its long journey home, manned by just a twenty-five-person maintenance crew. The trip to Earth would take the better part of a year, but the vessel was just too valuable to leave permanently on Mars station. It would return to the Red Planet again on Expedition IV along with its sister vessels, bringing reinforcements of ships, troops, equipment, and supplies two years hence.

Becky, Mellie, and I watched our slow approach to Phobos on the viewscreen in our cramped cabin. Once more we were in "lockdown" or "safe" mode, with all of the airtight doors throughout the vessel being snugly secured in the event of sudden attack. The Martian moon, a large meteor really, just drifted closer and closer, the bulk of the planet it orbited being gradually blocked from our vision, until we nudged up close against the docks awaiting us.

"It's good to see something solid again," Becky said.

"Yeah, but it's not much better than empty space," I said.

Phobos is a gray-colored, elliptical-shaped planetoid almost seventeen miles long, densely covered with craters, including one massive structure that clearly shows the cracking caused by the ancient impact on its surface. Like its smaller sister satellite, Deimos, it always displays the same face towards Mars. The gravity of the moon is so slight that everything on the Base must be anchored to its surface, lest a kick or a touch dislodge it into empty space. The original survey team in Year Six had very carefully used parts of the supply ships that had accompanied that mission to establish a permanent port facility on the surface, reworking the cargo containers into a chain of heavily-shielded, interconnected living quarters and storage facilities that were firmly bolted into the rock. These had been augmented by several small excavations into the moon itself, and by multiple emplacements of defensive missiles and lasers.

We were greeted personally by the Base Commander, Colonel Rufus "Rufe" Choate, and escorted to temporary communal lodgings. It would take three days of continual effort to unburden the great spacecraft of its supplies, but in the end the *Armageddon* would also set sail for Earth, making way for the third of the expedition's ships to offload its passengers and cargo—the great French vessel, *Le Fléau*. Similar efforts were occurring on Deimos, where some of the smaller members of the fleet began disembarking their precious supplies, reinforcing the human complement there, and augmenting its weaponry, basic amenities, and living accommodations.

We'd just reached our new quarters when the klaxons sounded.

"Orange Alert!" blared the loudspeakers.

We were under attack again!

We quickly strapped ourselves into our hammocks. I could feel the thump-thump-thump vibrations in the wall from the launching of the missiles. I couldn't reach our com set, so we were completely blind and dumb as to what was happening around us in space.

"Daddy, I'm scared!" Mellie said.

I reached out and held her hand. It was all I could do. Becky comforted her on the other side.

When the "All Clear" signal sounded several hours later, I released myself and immediately turned on the set.

"Central Command has confirmed," the announcer said, "that Phobos Base was attacked by three Martian ships similar in configuration to those that originally landed on Earth. They apparently were launched quite some time ago from an unknown alien base in the Asteroid Belt, and were far enough off the plane of Mars's orbit that none of our scanners picked them up until just before the assault. All of the alien vessels have now been destroyed or neutralized.

"One attacker was downed by the Warstation *San Bernardino*, firing from Mars orbit. Some of the fragments of the destroyed craft impacted on Barracks C-8 and C-9, killing twenty people there. A second invader was sufficiently damaged by our Base defenses that it was sent whirling off into space. The third alien damaged the communications array on the *Thunderbolt* with its sting-ray before being rammed by the pod *Albert Einstein*, piloted by Lt. Andrew Kapel, who died in the head-on crash. We're assured by Col. Morris, Captain of the *Thunderbolt*, that that vessel can and will be promptly repaired.

"General Burgess has released a statement commending our brave troops for their vigilance, and vowing to eliminate the Martian menace once and for all."

This statement was rerun every few minutes throughout the next day.

But when we joined some of the other families and our friends in the mess hall, we heard a very different story. The Base Commander was reportedly furious over the failure of our tracking teams to pick up the incoming aliens until just a few moments before they hit. The third Martian had apparently intended to smash its craft into the center of our complex, and only the quick thinking and selfless sacrifice of the pod pilot had saved the facility from major, perhaps irreparable damage. Once again we'd been lucky. The officer in charge of the radar emplacements had been reassigned.

Thereafter things quieted again. One by one the major ships of the fleet were maneuvered into the docking facilities on both satellites, until the moons were each completely covered with storage bunkers and materiel on the sides facing away from Mars. More facilities and containers were erected in quick order, and these too were rapidly filled to the brim. By this time the several hundred smaller supply shuttles and pods were also beginning to make their appearances in Mars orbit; these were simply anchored together in space, being partially shadowed by the two moons and protected by our defensive Warstations. Eventually, they would be maneuvered to land on the planet itself, providing future living quarters and base camps for the settlers there.

Becky and Mellie and I had to share our quarters with two other families; we could only use our sleeping hammocks for eight hours a day before they had to be vacated and filled by other warm bodies. The situation became so crowded on Phobos Base that there was nothing to do but seek out whatever open space we could locate and then stay put for hours at a time. We spent our days talking to whomever passed us by. The Advisory Council had yet to be convened since our arrival, and we heard no news whatever about the progress of the war. I had absolutely nothing to occupy my time, and no access to any communication nodes.

I encountered Mindon a day or two later in the commissary or mess hall. The food on the Base was uniformly bad. We just had tubes of water to wash it down, and not much of that.

"You still having dreams?" he asked, as he pulled himself down next to me with his bottle of lunch.

"Off and on," I said. "They're never the same, and they're hard to describe. Some of them are so strange that it's as if I've been transported to Never-Never Land."

"It must be the Martians."

"That's what I thought too, but some of these dreams, Mindon, some of them can't possibly be scenes from or in Mars. They're just too weird. I mean, we're talking about floating giants and bizarre colors and fiery vistas, all in vivid, three-dimensional forms. It doesn't fit."

"Then what could they be?"

"I really have no idea," I said, "but some of the others are having them too. It has to mean something, although damned if I know what. And why me?"

Geoff Alexander then pulled himself over to us.

"What is this goop, anyway?" he asked, holding up a plastic

squeeze bottle of something that looked like a cross between oatmeal and the "green slime."

"Some kind of puréed vegetable?" Mindon said.

"It's neither vegetable nor animal nor mineral," I said, "and it doesn't taste very good either."

"You would have thought that, having traveled all this distance, we could have done something a little better than gory goo or grokky glop," Geoff said.

"Yeah," we both chimed in.

"We were just talking about Alex's dreams," Mindon said. "Has anyone made an effort to record these things or compare them in any way?"

"Not to my knowledge," I said.

"Well, maybe they ought to. Maybe the Martians or whoever are trying to tell us something. Maybe this is the way they communicate."

"I can't believe that. It would be terribly inefficient, among other things, and from what I observed of the aliens on Earth, they were always efficient."

"Still."

"Let's bring it up at the next Council meeting," Geoff said, putting his container away. "Gad, I can't take any more of this crap. Nothing but the green grog morning, noon, and night. At this pace, I'm going to lose weight, guys."

"Yeah," we all said in unison, and then we went our separate ways again.

CHAPTER TEN
DOWN TO "EARTH"

If I had not been there I should have been very much bored.
—Charles Copeland

ALEX SMITH, 7 BI-AUGUST, MARS YEAR VII
PHOBOS BASE, IN ORBIT AROUND PLANET MARS

General Burgess called a meeting of the Advisory Council at 0900 Phobos time on August the Seventh. By then things were getting downright crowded on both of the moon bases, with people and their belongings and foodstuffs and military equipment crammed into every crack and corner of the establishment. Clearly, this could not continue much longer. Folks were getting very, very cranky.

"It's time to move on, ladies and gentlemen," the General announced, his voice being carried on a live feed to all the remaining ships and bases. "It's time to take the war to the enemy! It's time to launch Operation Crimson Storm!"

Everyone began cheering enthusiastically, and it continued for at least five minutes.

"We've been real lucky so far," the officer said. "Sure, we've suffered our share of losses, but overall we've come through the initial stage of our mission better than expected. We thought we'd have fewer resources available to us at this point.

"But we shouldn't kid ourselves, folks. Right now we've occupied Martian 'airspace' with an overwhelming force. We knew we could do this successfully, if the aliens hadn't developed any new weapons during the last few years. That's why we dispatched Expeditions I and II, to learn some of these things in advance, to make certain we wouldn't be surprised.

"But once we actually land on Mars, all bets are off. We've realized from our experience on Earth that the Martians are tough, disciplined fighters who rarely make the same mistakes twice. Their technology is at least as good as ours, if not better. We've adapted some of their leftover hardware for our own use, and we know a lot more about the aliens than we did a dozen years ago—but that doesn't mean this is going to be a walk in the park.

"Remember, we not only have to defeat the enemy, we must also occupy the dry, desolate world down there and make a life for ourselves—and this for a period of at least two years, until reinforcements arrive. No one's going to rescue us if we run out of food, water, air, medications, or weapons. No one's going to save us from our own mistakes—or from the Martians either. We're completely on our own now.

"So let's get out there and do what needs to be done! Let's take the battle to the enemy!"

More cheering. Hell, we were all flag-wavers at this point.

"Now let me introduce Dr. Asaph Halleran, who will give us some background information on the planet."

Halleran was a member of Mindon's group of scientists. He was a punctilious little man of about fifty with a face like an aged bulldog's.

"Mars is about half the size of Earth," he said, "with a gravity about two-fifths of our own planet. Its rotation period, its day, is roughly equivalent to our own, as is the total usable land area. Its year is twice as long as ours. Mars has two polar caps that are sometimes covered with dry ice and sometimes with frozen water. The average temperature on the planet is about minus sixty degrees Fahrenheit, but occasional spikes can reach just as far in the other direction at low spots on the Martian Equator. The atmosphere is mostly carbon dioxide, and very, very thin by our standards. The absence of a thick atmospheric shell means that solar radiation is an ever-present danger: you must all be constantly aware of the hazard."

His face on the base com screens was replaced with a panoply of the Martian surface; to those of us who were physically present he just unrolled a wall map.

"Now, if you'll look very closely at this image before you"— he pointed to the map—"you'll see this large dark area on the top of the planet surrounding its North Pole. This great northern plain, the Vastitas Borealis, represents, we believe, the bed of an ancient Martian ocean, a uniformly low and relatively level region where the vast majority of the alien bases have been identified. Most are located in large craters such as Korolev and Lomonosov. We think they may all be interlinked with tunnel systems.

"Thus far we've identified no Martian emplacement below forty-five degrees north latitude, the southernmost base being located in the Nier Crater in the Utopia Planitia plain, around forty-seven degrees."

"Thank you, Dr. Halleran," the General said. "Comments, anyone?"

"How do you know these are actual bases?" I asked.

"Well, they all had weapons emplacements," Burgess said, "and when they fired on us, they were targeted by our Warstations from orbit. All now appear to have been put out of commission."

"How many were there?"

"Uhhh…."

"There were seven, General," his adjutant, Major Petrie Q. Levine, said.

"So where are the Martians themselves?" I said.

There was a moment of complete silence.

"We don't know for sure." Burgess frowned.

"See, that's the problem I have here. I've sometimes been accused of piling speculation upon speculation, but isn't that what you folks are doing? We've located a half dozen Martian weapons 'pits,' for want of a better word, since that's what I think these are; and we're assuming from these small discoveries that the Martians live mostly on the northern plains. Maybe they do, gentlemen, but where's your evidence?"

No one had any answers, of course, and we went 'round and 'round the mess hall tables until it was dinnertime again, and we had to vacate the area.

We needed to decide, and relatively soon, where we would concentrate our forces on the surface, and which of the Martian structures we would try to attack or infiltrate. We had limited fuel and limited military resources and limited supplies with which to establish *our* permanent bases on the surface; we couldn't afford to waste our efforts and still have any realistic chance of success.

Mars was a big place, we were discovering, and there were so many possible choices, so many potential mishaps, that we were almost to the point of being "damned if we do" and "damned if we don't."

I looked again at an atlas of the Red Planet. Where, how, when, and why were the constant questions that continually plagued those of us actively involved in planning this enterprise.

I suddenly found Zee, of all people, looking over my shoulder. He stabbed one blunt, scarred finger down at a crater in the central part of Utopia Planitia.

"N-nier t-to-d-day," he stammered. "G-gone t-tomorrow!"

CHAPTER ELEVEN
DOWN TO "MARS"

Flout 'em, and scout 'em, and scout 'em, and flout 'em.
—William Shakespeare

ALEX SMITH, 27 BI-AUGUST, MARS YEAR VII
PHOBOS BASE, IN ORBIT AROUND PLANET MARS

The rest of the fleet continued to arrive in Mars orbit, so that now we had almost all of our supply pods and supplemental vessels available to us. However, there was no place to put them other than stacked up in the space surrounding the two moons. They just hung there in clusters, their crews consuming irreplaceable supplies, waiting for a decision by the top brass. Something had to break very soon.

On the Fifteenth a riot broke out in the mess hall on Deimos Base, which, if anything, was now even more crowded than Phobos. I'm not sure if the protesters were expressing any specific grievances beyond the lousy food and generally cramped accommodations, but tensions were running high everywhere from the overcrowding.

Down on the planet, however, things had become almost funereally quiet. If the Martians were actively preparing a few surprises for our arrival, we certainly couldn't detect anything with our sensors. We bombarded the surface continually with radar, but found nothing new. We also continued to have regular, almost daily meetings of the Advisory Council, but little ever seemed to be decided. Finally General Burgess called us together again on the Twenty-Seventh.

"I want to thank everyone for their input," he said. "I've made a decision. We're landing at two places, folks: on the Isidis Planitia plain southwest of Nier Crater, and at the Granicus Valles area in Utopia Planitia, southeast of Nier. We'll commence operations at 0600 on September the First, four days hence."

I raised my hand.

"Dr. Smith."

"I take it that Nier Crater is our primary target," I said.

"Initially, yes, but I also intend to move very quickly on the other known alien bases."

I made no further comment, since I had no more information than anyone else about the subject. It's just that I was uncomfortable somehow with this particular choice, and I couldn't really understand why. I hadn't been feeling very well for many days now. The base food disagreed with me, and my incessant dreams kept me tossing and turning each night in a frenzy of I-don't-know-what. They were just disturbing, that's all. And I knew that Becky and Mellie were experiencing many of the same things.

That morning my eyes had looked bloodshot to me, and I'd gone to the Base Infirmary, where I had to wait two hours to see a treatment nurse. She gave me some antacids for the digestive problems, and some drops for my eyes ("the air's very dry in this self-contained environment, you know"). I thought about seeing the local shrink over my recurring nightmares, but when I learned that she had a waiting list of over a month, I demurred. I felt this underlying sense of disquiet.

"It's like someone's running their fingernails over a blackboard," Mindon said one day at breakfast.

"Breakfast" in this case consisted of some weak orange juice in a tube, and a choice between semi-liquefied eggs or gray cereal in a squeeze bottle. The menu was always the same: "puréed shit," everyone called it.

"I'm sick of this!" someone shouted across the room.

"Me too!" yelled another.

"I want some decent food!" a third voice said.

"How about what the officers get!" another man said.

"Yeah!" Everyone chimed in. "Yeah!"

Then General Burgess showed up and pulled himself into the open where everyone could see, hanging up there near the ceiling. He held up his orange drink in one hand and a tube of eggs in another, just like all the rest of us, and quietly performed an aerial pirouette.

"Don't eat any different than the rest of you," he said in his gravelly voice. "Never have, never will. We're all in this together. Things'll be better when we're down on the surface, believe me. We'll be able to set up our hydroponics labs again, just like we had on the transports. Fresh food for everyone. All for one and one for all, that's the way it works, ladies and gents. The only people here who get any preferences are the children. They need special nutrients to grow and develop properly, and so I make sure they get them. But the rest of you—well, enjoy your breakfast!"

The man had a knack, I had to admit. They cheered him over and over again as he took his place right among them. He never ate alone in his cubicle or with his officers, and he also picked a different group each time to share his meals with. It gave the average "Joe" the chance to voice his or her complaints directly to the top man.

"So I guess they must shit brown just like the rest of us, too," Mindon muttered.

I choked on my eggs, and it took me several minutes to regain my composure, hacking and sneezing while I fought for my breath. Then I saw my friend's eyes narrow for a moment and look right past me. A short figure with dark hair swung down beside him on the other side.

"Nomsah!" he said.

"Hey, Min." She leaned over and brushed his cheek.

Then she turned the dark orbs of her eyes directly on me.

"Dr. Alex Smith, I presume. We meet again, just as I

predicted."

"Madame Stavroula." I bowed my forehead. "'You've come a long way, baby.'"

She shook her head.

"You men are so predictable," she said. "Every *cliché* in the book, but you still rattle them out nonetheless, as if we're impressed by such things. I hear you're having a few bad dreams."

"Yeah, a few, but nothing that need concern you."

"Oh, *I'm* not concerned," she said. "I know that *you* know everything you need to about such matters. You *are* looking a little gray around the gills these days, though. I like the red eyes: that's a very distinctive touch."

"Now, now, children," Mindon said, "be nice to each other. We don't want to start another fracas in the pub, do we?"

I concentrated for a moment on my delectable delights, forcing myself to swallow some of the library paste they were passing off for food.

"Why...?" I started to say, but suddenly thought better of it.

"Why am I here?" she asked. "Or why are *you* here? I think the answers to both questions are somehow the same. I think the universe has brought us to this special place at this particular time for a purpose. I'm not sure yet what that purpose is."

"I don't really believe in purposes," I said.

"That doesn't matter, Alex Smith. *They* do. *They* planted the seeds. *They* brought us here. But they're so different from us that any communication is shadowy at best. What you see at night are their minds reaching out to you."

"But some of what I experience is so *outré*," I said, "that it can't possibly derive from Mars, at least not under any circumstance that I can imagine."

"But how do you actually know that? You've spent your life making assumptions, Alex, many of which have been proven wrong. I've read your book. You've acknowledged that your judgments about the Martians during the original invasion of Earth were based on misapprehension. So, what's different now?

"And even if what you say is true in one sense or another, in that it accurately and objectively reflects your experiences, where exactly *is* the truth in that? What *are* you actually seeing? Maybe there's something greater here that has yet to be grasped by any of us."

"Maybe, maybe, maybe!" I said.

I was suddenly furiously angry at her, at myself, at my wife again, at everyone on the expedition.

"There are *never* any answers with you people, never any resolutions. I'm tired of this uncertainty. I'm tired of grasping at philosophical straws. I want to know."

Zee came floating by right then, and Nomsah gently brought him to a halt above us.

"This man wants some answers," the fortune teller said to him, while nodding at me.

He looked down at us, framed against the light like some ancient god of yore, his hair all akimbo, his head shining with the reflected glow.

"I-I h-have t-too m-many o-of t-them," he said, before vanishing in the haze.

CHAPTER TWELVE
THE MARTIAN WAY

Go where we will on the surface of things,
men will have been there before us.
—Henry David Thoreau

ALEX SMITH, 1 BI-SEPTEMBER, MARS YEAR VII
U.S.S. GEORGE A. CUSTER, IN TRANSIT TO PLANET MARS

Our first sight of Mars, as the shuttle *Custer* swept down from Phobos Base, was utterly breathtaking. We could see the ochre color of the place in all its splendor, a white, irregular blob of ice marking its South Pole, like a small hat adorning a "funny face."

Phobos is so close to its primary that the Red Planet quickly occupies the entire landscape of one's vision, filling it up with a ruddy-orange glow, giving everything within the cabin of the shuttle a sickly rose hue.

"Hang on, folks," the pilot yelled over the com. "It's going to get a little rough down here."

We were starting to brush the top of Mars's thin atmosphere. The pilot tilted our craft upwards to take the brunt of the heat generated by the friction of the air on the ship's coated belly. I could see tiny pieces of fuselage breaking away and flicking back by the windows, little streaks of bright light championing our arrival in a flurry of colorful fireworks.

I knew that several other shuttles and pods were following us at a respectful distance, and that a half dozen of the little ships had already preceded us earlier that day on the short journey to Isidis Planitia. General Burgess had flown with that initial group of vessels, flanked by a pair of specially equipped fighting craft armed with missiles and lasers.

Now I could hear the whistling of our passage as we rushed towards our landing site. The entire shuttle seemed to rock and rattle, up and down, up and down, giving me a faint tinge of nausea.

"I feel a little sick, Daddy," my daughter said.

"It'll pass," I said. "There's a bag in the compartment right in front of you if you need to throw up."

Becky squeezed my hand hard. We were on our way to our new home.

Before embarking on the expedition to Mars, I'd retired from the California State University System, and Becky had taken a leave of absence from her editorial post for a local publishing house, Freon Books. We'd debated selling our house in Novato, but had finally decided to lease it to a fellow faculty member and his Significant Other, with an option to buy the place if we decided not to return. Housing was so expensive in California that I didn't want to burn all of our bridges too soon. Most of our personal belongings we'd put in storage, since we could take very little with us.

Through the narrow side windows of our shuttle we could see the planet rapidly moving towards us. Every second revealed new details of Mars's surface: huge craters, long canyons, streaks of dust and color, flat plains, enormous mountains, and rocks galore. Suddenly there was a bright flash of light.

"What was that?" someone yelled.

"We're receiving incoming," the pilot shouted over the com, "taking evasive maneuvers—now!"

The craft abruptly rolled right and then left, and then right again. Another flash lit up the interior of the shuttle. Suddenly I saw a third streak slant down from above, impacting with a large explosion somewhere on the surface of the planet to the north.

"They got it!" I heard.

It'd all happened so quickly that it was over and done with before we barely realized what was occurring.

We passed over some mountains and then leveled off. The Seabees had already cleared one long runway for the shuttles by the time we got to Isis Station, moving all the loose sand off to one side; they were now working on a second strip with their stunted, odd-looking, fully-enclosed bulldozers. They'd make it a more secure and stable structure later on, I was sure, but right now it looked like heaven's gate. We settled down with nary a bump, gradually coming to a slow halt.

A tractor hitched itself to the front of our ship, and began pulling it off the landing strip. As soon as we were clear, another shuttle coasted down right behind us, and another, and so on, continuing throughout the next week on a twenty-four-hour-per-day basis.

We were pulled over to a partially enclosed stone bunker, where we were left alone for several hours. This was standard procedure in those early days; I knew that some of the shuttles would have to remain where they were for quite some time. However, we were used to the cramped quarters on Phobos Base, and so we simply set up shop, helping our fellow passengers get situated, and employing the com screens to follow current developments. We had food and air and water and rough entertainment sufficient to last us a week, if necessary, plus several of the less discussed but utterly necessary amenities. The shuttle roof provided enough protection from the solar radiation to allow us to survive for a few weeks at least.

Most of us just sat up and stretched for the first time since we'd left Earth—and a few of us then sat right down again, not being used to the increased weight. Even though the gravity of Mars was only thirty-eight percent of Earth's, the sudden pressure on our bones and cardiovascular systems left some of us gasping for more than a few moments.

I suddenly felt my age for the very first time in my life, and

I knew right then that I couldn't go home again. By the time I'd spent a few years here, my skeleton wouldn't be able to adapt to Earth's stronger gravitational force.

For better or worse, *this* was now our home.

"Daddy, look!" Mellie exclaimed, pointing out one of the portholes.

I saw a large white container dangling from a set of parachutes, slowly making its way down to the surface of the plain in the distance—I don't know how far. The horizon here was closer than it would have been on Earth, and it took me a long time to be able to judge such things accurately.

Then another half dozen sugar cubes sprinkled themselves over the ochre terrain, and then a third set; and soon the red sands of Mars were glittering with the jewels of our future homes and supplies. Some of them even piled down upon each other, resting at odd angles on the sandy soil. The containers were designed to be used, emptied, and then reconverted into living and storage spaces for the base, once we prepared dugouts for them. Ultimately, they would have to be placed underground and covered over with layers of rock and soil to provide additional protection against the sun.

I knew that something similar was happening many miles away to the east at Granick Valley on the edge of the great Utopia Planitia expanse.

The Seabees, as usual, were Johnny-on-the-spot. A company of the construction workers had disembarked from the very first shuttle, and had immediately begun offloading the equipment they needed from the initial pods. Piece by meticulous piece they began assembling their gear, using specially designed machines to clear roads and runways, set up fields of solar cells, erect living and storage facilities, and move the shuttles and pods into their respective positions. I think that most of these guys and gals worked for two days straight without taking any rest. They were a key element to the quick establishment of our surface presence on the Red Planet.

It was dark before they came for us. A kind of enclosed-cab

electric tractor pulling a box behind it rumbled up close by our craft. Two men in environmental suits got out and maneuvered the rear structure so that it "mated" with our airlock. Then the thing cycled through, and we were taken out in groups of fifteen or twenty at a time.

Our initial destination was a windowless pod standing off to one side, part of a cluster of such structures situated a half mile from the runway. It was already buried up to its roof, although not yet covered with Martian "earth," as it would be within the next week.

We followed the same procedure as before, linking with the lock attached to the top edge of the pod to allow us finally to disembark. We had to step one by one down a narrow, winding metal staircase into the structure itself.

The interior of the cube was a maze of storage bins and rough living quarters. We were given an open cubicle with a number splashed in alabaster over the doorway, and handed three hammocks and a rough curtain to draw across the entrance for privacy. That was it. A common mess hall would be established between the pods within a few days, linked to them by solid concrete corridors built into specially cut ditches; in the meantime, we were stuck surviving with the wretched MREs, of which there was quite literally a ton piled all around us in the bins.

I had serious trouble walking the few hundred feet from the entrance to our new "bedroom." Becky helped me maintain my slow, weary pace, and she and Mellie had to set up the basic arrangement of our new home, because I was so exhausted that I could barely move. I was beginning to wonder if I would ever adapt to the Martian gravity.

But my womenfolk nudged me into my swing-swing-swinging bed, and before I could even comment or object or say "boo," before I could even prognosticate again, I fell into a deep, dark, bottomless sleep.

* * * * * * *

Once again we were sloshing about in our pool of salt water, drifting with the slow movement of its washing waves.

We yearned most piteously for some resolution to the pain that filled us from within.

All the chaos, all the unrest, disrupted our well-being, disturbed the nest. The weed caressed our bodies, but gave no surcease.

We blended with its narh, *but gained slack comfort from our efforts.*

The kol-qah *lent us their life force, but their essence tasted of bile and bitterroot.*

We reached out for aid to our trusty nest-companions, but none responded to our entreaties.

We cried out for help with all of our being.

Where were they, our lost bud-brothers? Why had they abandoned us?

Speak to us, oh wise, wide wights of the ancient-ones!

Sing to us your songs of grief and graciousness!

"Ooh-lah!" we did howl to the eldest of the eld, "Ooh-lah!"

PART TWO
MARS DESCENDENT

What things we have seen
Done at the Mermaid! heard words that have
   been
So nimble, and so full of flame,
As if that everyone from whence they came,
Had meant to put his whole wit in a jest,
And resolved to live a fool, the rest
Of his dull life.
                 —Francis Beaumont

There Leviathan
Hugest of living creatures, on the deep
Stretched like a promontory sleeps or swims,
And seems a moving land, and at his gills
Draws in, and at his trunk spouts out a sea.
                 —John Milton

CHAPTER THIRTEEN
THE CREAM OF THE JEST

A Funny Thing Happened on the Way to the Forum.
—Larrah Gelbart & Burt Shrevelove

ALEX SMITH, 8 BI-SEPTEMBER, MARS YEAR VII
ISIS STATION, PLANET MARS

Gradually I regained my strength over the next week. By the third day I was able to walk short distances again, and to involve myself once more in the affairs of our little colony.

The Isidis Planitia area is a very large and ancient circular crater about 930 miles in diameter, located right on the southeastern edge of the Utopia Planitia plain. It appears to have been an ancient bay or lake, possibly connected to the larger ocean bed just to the north, although a ridge of higher land separates the two regions; the latter may possibly represent a continuation of the Nepenthas Mensae mountain range. The Nier Crater was located about 1,400 miles to the northeast of Isidis, which is the genitive case in Latin of the Egyptian goddess Isis (in English the area would be called the "Isis Plain").

Isidis was picked partially for its location, and partly because it was the original target of the Beagle 2 Mars probe that had been lost in 2003. Some researchers now believe that it was the alien discovery of that mission (and their possible destruction of the satellite) that triggered the original Martian invasion of Earth. We were only a short distance from the wreckage of the probe that had been spotted years before from Mars orbit.

Slowly the Isis Station began to take shape. The supply pods were gradually moved one by one to their final resting places, where they were buried and anchored securely *in situ*. The residential areas were organized around sections, barracks, and blocks, each of them bearing large, distinctive, glowing white numerals and letters painted on their tops and locks.

The individual barracks buildings were arranged in groups called sections, which were designated by different letters of the alphabet. The sections themselves featured a separate mess hall or cafeteria erected in the middle of the complex, together with communal shower facilities. Water was in very short supply, and individuals were only allowed to bathe once a month—and then only for a few seconds. All waste was recycled.

Within each barrack, families or "pairs" were given cubicles numbered consecutively within each building. Unmarried or unattached individuals had to share a cubicle with someone else, the only exceptions being senior officers or staff, or those few with serious health problems.

The entire residential area also had a medical pod, serving all of the sections, with nurses and doctors and psychologists on duty twenty-four hours per day. Minor and major injuries were common as the complex was being constructed.

Everything was connected with underground passageways, linked together from prefabricated sections unloaded from the original transport vessels or special supply pods, and then sealed tightly against the elements and shielded against the solar radiation. Nonetheless, airtight doors and airlocks were everywhere present, and there were specific protocols required of all visitors to sections and buildings other than their own.

The command post was built in similar fashion, as were the military facilities, large supply warehouses, external hangers for aircraft, shuttles, and machines, the hydroponics labs, and the outlying defensive emplacements, which included the usual complement of missiles and lasers. Later enhancements featured extensive minefields surrounding the entire encampment, better runways, emergency lighting, a small nuclear power plant, several fields of solar cells (although the power generated from these was small, they provided a continuous daily augmentation to our energy needs), and lightweight windmills to generate electricity from both small and great movements of the thin Martian atmosphere. Wells were dug, but no water was found in the immediate vicinity.

A week after our landing, I accompanied General Burgess on our first extensive trip outside Isis Station, an expedition to the crash site of the Beagle 2 probe some twenty-five miles distant. We used some specially adapted half-track vehicles designed specifically for travel on the sandy Martian terrain (in the mountainous areas, we employed an entirely different set of transports). The half-tracks had roofs that provided extra shielding from the ever-present radiation, but even so, there were strict protocols that governed the amount of time any individual could spend on the surface of the planet.

Everywhere around us were seemingly endless vistas of red rocks and dunes and the rises caused by great and small meteor impacts from the distant past. Nowhere did we spot any signs of life.

The probe was where it was supposed to be, scattered in pieces along a mile-deep corridor of debris.

"Not much left, is there?" one of the officers muttered into his com.

"No, it's pretty well destroyed," a female voice said.

Several of us obtained permission to exit the vehicles, outfitted in environmental suits configured to provide oxygen and heat and water (and solar protection!) in the harsh climate of the Red Planet. The temperature outside, I was later told, was about twenty degrees Fahrenheit, quite a warm day on Mars.

I slowly trudged over to the major remaining section of the Beagle 2 craft (I was not yet back to full strength), and bent over slightly to examine what had obviously been a communication array, huffing a little to regain my breath.

"Look here!" I said. "This burnt area suggests that the probe was hit with a sting-ray while it was descending."

"The marks could also have been caused by the atmosphere if the satellite had descended too quickly," Lieutenant Harlan said.

"I don't think so," I said. "I saw these markings back on Earth during the War of Two Worlds. They're very distinctive."

And then I noticed something odd off to the northern side of the site. I shuffled across the crimson surface maybe fifty or hundred feet, stirring up the dust as I went, until I reached a low rise overlooking the area.

"Uh, General, I think you better see this!"

He and his entourage joined me. I pointed down, and didn't need to say anything further.

Coming towards us from the uncertain distant horizon was a set of large, deep tracks, quite evenly spaced and partially filled in, that ended right where I stood, and then obviously retraced their steps back towards the same direction. I'd seen these markings many times before.

They were the footprints left by a great Martian tripod fighting-machine!

CHAPTER FOURTEEN
GIANTS UNLEASHED

Traveling is a fool's paradise....
My giant goes with me wherever I go.
—Ralph Waldo Emerson

ALEX SMITH, 15 BI-SEPTEMBER, MARS YEAR VII
ISIS STATION, PLANET MARS

The discovery that the aliens had visited the Beagle 2 crash site was profoundly disturbing to everyone on the expedition, but left us with very few new answers. We now knew or strongly suspected that the enemy had destroyed the probe, and had sent one of their striders to investigate the wreck; but we had no notion really whence the great strider had derived. After salvaging a piece of the broken frame, General Burgess ordered the tractors to return to base.

Where were the Martians?

The question plagued the joint meetings of the Expedition III Advisory Council, which had now been re-established at both stations, and linked through videoconferencing. Some of the officers and advisers recommended an immediate assault on the alien facility at Nier Crater, the closest known site of a Martian compound, while others urged caution.

Hampering all of our decisions was a decided lack of information and mobility. The Seabees were still assembling major portions of the infrastructures of both our two stations, Isis and Granick Valley, and hadn't yet begun putting together the specially designed flying machines that we intended to use to scout the Martian positions. The orbital shuttles employed irreplaceable rocket fuel, and were needed to transport men and materiel to and from our moon bases and satellite Warstations. Deploying them for routine surface surveillance was impractical save in an emergency, and the view from our satellites sometimes failed to provide enough surface detail to allow the appropriate context for their observations.

Ground movement of our troops was a slow and cumbersome business. Our transport half-tracks could safely average no more than ten or fifteen miles per hour in the rough, rocky, ungraded terrain that filled the dry beds of the Red Planet's ancient ocean basins. The motors depended on batteries that were recharged daily from banks of solar cells that tended to get very dusty in the course of travel, and had to be wiped clean constantly in order to generate enough power to keep the tractors moving. Their engines were sealed against the dirt, but required considerable maintenance to avoid overstraining their components. Wheel bearings had to be pulled and serviced at least once weekly when in heavy use.

But where were the Martians?

No attacks had been made on any of our facilities since our arrival on the planet. Were the aliens waiting for us to advance against their pits? I knew from my experience with the creatures on Earth during the War of Two Worlds that they were inherently cautious, and tended to wait until they could evaluate the appropriate response to a particular threat before taking action, and I said so.

"We can't just sit here indefinitely, sir," Major Levine said. "We have to move aggressively against the enemy."

"How long before we have aerial surveillance capabilities?" Burgess asked.

"We launched the first drone earlier this morning, sir. We're following the tripod tracks in the sand back to its origin. I've got a live feed, if you want to see what's happening."

"Put it on the screen."

"Yes, sir."

Then we saw a video image of the Martian desert from a height of about 100 feet. Slowly but steadily the ruddy terrain continued to unfurl before our eyes, consisting mostly of rocks and sand. I'd actually seen the flying machine before it was launched: it had a pair of oversized propellers, long, narrow wings, and a needle-like body, all fashioned of lightweight composite materials. It was ideal to navigate the thin Martian atmosphere.

"Where's the craft now?" the General asked.

Levine checked with one of his aides.

"We're just beyond the edge of Isidis Planitia, sir," he said, "moving into Utopia Planitia, heading generally northeast."

"Towards Nier Crater?"

"It appears so, sir."

"Any signs of other tracks or activity by the enemy?"

"Not so far, sir."

"Very well, then. Let us know when you find something further."

So where were the Martians?

We came to no other conclusions during our afternoon meeting, which ended with the General wishing his wife happy birthday, all of the delegates joining in to cheer her sudden appearance. She beamed at the attention she was getting. Then we went off as a group to a celebratory supper.

With the hydroponics facility recently inaugurated, we were able to champion Mrs. Dalpha Burgess's natal day with a very small handful of greens, the first of the fresh produce that was available. It wasn't much, but after more than a month of eating MREs and tube tripe, even these few bites seemed like ambrosia. The lab not only provided essential food and nutrients for the colony, but also generated oxygen, a byproduct of the plant growth. The positive benefits to camp morale were even more significant.

However, we still needed to locate a source of water on the

planet. The supplies that we'd brought with us from Earth were limited. Although we recycled everything as much as was realistically possible, a little bit of moisture was lost every time one of us exited through the airlocks into the Martian atmosphere. Burgess had already dispatched several two-man exploration teams into the surrounding mountain ranges, but nothing had been found as yet.

Where were the Martians?

I pondered that question again as I settled into my hammock that evening. What did the aliens actually think of us? How did they perceive our presence here? Other than that one set of tracks, and the handful of military responses that had been made from the Martian pit emplacements, the Red Planet still looked mostly like a Dead Planet. We'd found very few signs of current activity. The Martians had to be tucked away somewhere, but where and how many?

"Alex, you're swinging again," Becky mumbled.

"What?" I said. "Oh, sorry, dear, didn't mean to wake you."

"I know you didn't mean to, but you did anyway. Go to sleep, dear."

"Yes, sir."

"What?"

"Yes, dear," I said more loudly.

Then she started snoring again. I wasn't far behind.

Sometime in the middle of the night, around 0300 in the morning, the klaxons, the damned alarms, began sounding again.

"What is it this time?" I muttered, half asleep, as I rolled out of my hammock.

Then a large "thump" shook the ground.

"Jesus!" I said. "Get up, everyone!"

I switched on the night light, dousing us in a pale glow of bilious yellow, and slipped a pair of jeans and a T-shirt over my underpants, and sandals on my feet. While my wife was dressing, I pulled out the emergency breathers for each of us, just in case.

"Mellie!" Becky was shouting. "She won't wake up, Alex!"

There was a large crash, the pod physically shuddered on its foundation, and the lights went out completely. Someone yelled for a medic, and a woman just began screaming her bloody head off in the distance. Suddenly I could smell smoke.

"Cripes," I said, grabbing my wife's hand and picking up my unconscious daughter.

"Alex?" Becky asked.

She knew that I had no business carrying any weight in my condition, but the adrenaline gave me the strength to sling Mellie over my back.

"Emergency evacuation!" the speakers ordered. "Barracks [crackle-crackle] through Seven of Section C, proceed at once to Section D. Repeat, [crackle]-acks Three through Seven of Section [crackle], proceed [crackle] to Section D. Repeat."

And it kept blaring its orders over and over again until it cut off in mid-crackle.

We were located in Block 38, Barrack 7 of Section C, and had practiced the evacuation drill several times before, our eyes shut tight to simulate a power outage. I led my family through the winding aisles of the storage pod, until we came to a place where the passageway was blocked by the overthrow of some of the unused goods. I was huffing and puffing by this time, and needed to stop anyway.

"What do we do now, Alex?" Becky asked.

"We go around," I said, and led them slowly back to the last cross junction.

The smoke was getting much worse by this point.

"Put on your masks," I ordered, when I felt my head beginning to spin, and waited until Becky had secured the thing over Mellie's face.

The breathers would give us emergency oxygen for a period of about thirty minutes, depending on our exertion level. They wouldn't protect us from the penetrating cold outside if the pods were breached, or from the effects of being exposed to the very low atmospheric pressure. Those would kill us long before we ran out of air!

My wife then took our daughter from my arms. I didn't try arguing with her. I was just too damned tired.

Another huge "thump" shook the entire pod, although it didn't appear to me actually to impact upon the structure.

Finally we reached the exit, where we had to wait in line for ten minutes before cycling through ourselves. The airlocks only allowed about ten people at a time to pass into the corridor linking our barrack with another in the chain.

There we were able to remove our breathers and store them again, with about ten or fifteen minutes of oxygen left in the small tanks. It took us another hour to reach Section D, where we crowded into Barrack 21.

By this time Mellie was awake again.

"What happened?" she asked.

"The Martians, I think," I said.

"Oh, I knew that," she said. "They all went away."

No one had many details of the attack. There had been no major breach in the pod structure, just a minor crack in one of the subterranean air lines. Then the ventilation system had partially failed due to a power breach elsewhere, and the pod had begun losing some of its warmth. A kind soul among the residents began passing out hot drinks, and someone else helped the less fortunate to bundle up against the creeping cold.

Hours later—a lifetime later it almost seemed to me—the "All Clear" signal sounded, but we had to remain in Section D for another half day, until our barrack was repaired. Finally we returned home. Other than some external scorching and a small internal fire, our pod was apparently still intact. Once the bins and power connections had been fixed and the air scrubbed of pollutants, we were back to "business as usual."

Except that it wasn't "usual" ever again, or at least not for a very long time: no one could sleep very well, except for Mellie. We all felt like targets now. We had to take action against the aliens before they returned again. But what could we do?

The next morning I toured the station with General Burgess

and other members of our Advisory Council. Several of the outlying laser sites had been destroyed, one of our pods had suffered a direct hit, with the loss of twenty civilians, and a hanger facility had been crumpled, although the shuttle housed within had survived with minimal damage and could still be salvaged. Most of the rest of the problems had been caused by power surges and overloads. I could see the ruins of a Martian fighting-machine slumped across Runway 1-R, Seabees and Marines and technicians and their equipment huddled around it, like surgeons at the operating table.

"What happened?" the General asked.

"Two striders, sir," came the response. "We got one for sure and may have damaged the other. It was approaching Section C of the Residential Compound when it abruptly turned tail and ran."

"How the hell did they get here, and how did we miss them in the first place?"

The words were shouted out.

"Don't know, sir," the soldier said.

"Well, you better bloody well find out, Private Gramlichen," Burgess said. "You'd better find out, and soon!"

CHAPTER FIFTEEN
DUNE BUGS

Soar into the air above the dunes.
—John Dos Passos

ALEX SMITH, 22 BI-SEPTEMBER, MARS YEAR VII
UTOPIA PLANITIA, PLANET MARS

Both Isis Station and Granick Valley had been simultaneously attacked in a beautifully coordinated effort. The damage
to our facilities was minimal; the damage to our psyches and to
our self-confidence was major. Somehow the aliens had slipped
through our net and caught us completely unawares. Somehow
they had shown an initiative and planning that was completely
different from what their operations had been like on Earth
years before.

Granick had lost several residential buildings and a hundred
precious lives, plus many supplies, including one of the pods of
irreplaceable water.

"We have to get more of the surveillance drones operational,"
General Burgess thundered at our next meeting of the Advisory
Council. "We have to know what happened, and we have to
keep it from ever happening again."

"Sir," Major Bethancourt said, "Drone Number 1 has finally
reached Nier Crater."

"What've you found?"

"The original fighting-machine's tracks lead right back to the

Martian emplacement. There are numerous other footprints of striders heading off from there in all directions, far too many for us to track. There's no sign of any surface activity or surviving Martian gun pits. I've redirected the flyer south to see if we can locate any prints of the four striders that attacked our stations."

"Thank you," Burgess said. "Ideas, anyone?"

"Sir, with all respect." It was Major Levine. "We have to get our personnel on site. We need to inspect the alien camp ourselves, and then assault and destroy it—the sooner, the better."

No one disagreed.

"Very well, go make it so," Burgess said. "The target date for departure is the Twenty-Second. Let's do it, folks!"

We assembled two strike forces, one at each station. The half-tracks would be slung under the bellies of specially modified shuttles and airlifted to Nier Crater. The Seabees worked furiously to assemble the equipment necessary for the twin missions, and also to construct more drones and flyers to provide cover for the strike, both through aerial surveillance and with their attack missiles.

The days just brushed past me in a gray blur. I managed to wangle an invitation to accompany Task Force I from Isis Station, but had to upgrade my basic weapons and survival training in order to qualify. As usual, Becky tried to talk me out of it.

"You've no business being involved in a military operation," she said. "You're no kid anymore, Alex. You're in your fifties, you've been sick, and you don't have the energy you did back on Earth."

All of this was quite true, of course, but my motivations were still the same as before.

"I have to see for myself," I said. "This is the first time that we've taken the war directly to the Martians, and I have to be there, Becky. It's historic. I want to be able to write about it first-hand."

My visions and my wild dreams had never gone away. I'd

been having them almost daily since we arrived on Mars. So had Becky and Mellie and a great many others, most of them women. I now believed that they were somehow tied to the squid-like creatures that we called the Martians. I was tired of being manipulated by politicians, government officials, and the aliens. I wanted to confront them myself. I simply had to be present when we attacked the alien pit. There was no question about it in my own mind, and I knew that nothing would deter me, now or in the future, except my own death—and God knows I'd thought about that possibility more than once in the last dozen years.

So, a week later and a dollar short I was bumping along in a half-track being swung through the air underneath one of the great shuttles. I could see the other vehicles on our mission being ferried along beside us, and the occasional shadow of a drone flying overhead as we neared the crater that honored the name of the late Alfred O. C. Nier, a well-known researcher in the study of meteors.

We were deposited on a level section of the Utopia Planitia basin about twenty miles southwest of the crater; our sister craft from Granick Valley were simultaneously landing about ten miles to the east of us. We would advance the next day on the surface in a joint pincher operation.

For now, though, we made temporary camp, piling up a berm around the vehicles and setting up a standard defensive perimeter. Most of us just stayed in our transports. We were dressed in warm clothing and boots against the cold Martian air, and had airtight environmental suits with breathers to cover our heads and provide radiation protection when we needed to venture outside. Sanitary facilities consisted of a hole in one of the vehicles covered by a heated portable latrine. Some noncom wag commented that we "wouldn't want to freeze our Privates off!"

It was while I was waiting in line at the Shitwagon, as we affectionately called it, that I ran into Private First Class Oliver Wendell Mayer. He recognized me immediately, although I didn't know him after all these years. He now sported a bushy, salt-and-pepper mustache.

"Dr. Smith!" he said. "Remember me? I was there at the first encounter with the Martians in Novato."

Now I knew him! It was the man who'd wanted to take human civilization into the sewers of San Francisco. We'd dogged each other throughout the War of Two Worlds.

"How're you doing, Mayer?" I asked, as the queue gradually advanced.

"Pretty damn good, sir. I joined up again as soon as I heard about this little excursion. I wanted to be there when we socked it to the Martians. They wouldn't have taken me normally—I'm too old—but since I'd had all that experience with the buggers in 'Frisco, they thought I might be useful. So here we are again, eh?"

"Here we are again," I said, and thought to myself that this was one encounter that I would have cheerfully forgone.

"Yeah, they made me a sergeant, but then I jimmied the toilet on the ship, and that cost me a stripe, and then, well, then I made goo-goo eyes at Lieutenant Cooper, and she started crying and all and put me on report again, so they took another, and now I'm back where I oughta be."

Truer words were never spoken. Then it was his turn at the toilet.

"No, you first, sir," he said most graciously. "I can wait."

"Thank you, Private," I said, and did my all for king and country.

I managed to avoid him for the rest of the day.

That evening we ate our MREs in our respective vehicles, and bunked down there for the night. At first light we were up again, and were ready to move shortly after dawn. We expected the trip to take two or three hours.

Both Task Forces started towards Nier simultaneously. The terrain here was typical of the Martian Planitiae: a little hilly in spots but relatively smooth, covered with ruddy gravel marred by a scattering of large and small rocks, interspersed with occasional dunes filled with blown sand that we usually tried to avoid if possible. There was nothing here that the half-tracks couldn't handle.

About halfway to the crater we encountered a line of hills that appeared to consist of loose soil or worse. The lead vehicle stopped suddenly.

"What's the problem?" General Burgess asked over the com.

"Uh, don't see any way 'round, sir," Captain Klinger said. "Surveillance indicates that the sand extends four or five miles in each direction."

"Can we get through?"

"I think so, sir. There's a sort of valley up here."

"Then proceed."

The first half-track moved out again, slowly approaching the declivity where a passage might be possible through the dunes. Just before it reached the edge of the sand, several of the hills began to heave upwards, and then the hoods of three Martian fighting-machines were visible, firing their sting-rays down at us. The lead transport melted into the ground, killing all of those aboard.

I don't know how the striders could move so quickly; perhaps it was because they'd been designed in the first place to operate in the unique environment of the Red Planet. Like the triangular heads of giant praying mantises, the hoods of the machines rapidly bobbed back and forth, shooting their rays of death at our expedition.

One of the drones soaring overhead fired a missile at the third strider, shattering one of its legs and toppling it to the ground; but before the flyer could unleash a second attack it was itself zapped by another fighting-machine and knocked from the sky, crashing nearby with a whump. Then the *San Francisco*, the Warstation positioned above us in Mars orbit, immediately joined the fray, and destroyed the remaining two Martian tripods without difficulty.

The hatch on the fallen machine abruptly popped open, and one of the aliens skittered out across the sand, moving rapidly sideways on its tentacles, much like a crab on Earth. It was covered with a skin-tight environmental suit. I had no idea that the Martians could race that fast. One of the lead half-tracks began firing at it, but the alien disappeared before it could be killed. The entire firefight had taken no more than five minutes.

Three of our vehicles and one drone were destroyed, and two other half-tracks were damaged; thirty-five of our troops died in the attack. We began getting similar reports from Task Force II to the east. The shuttles airlifted out the wounded and the bodies. Then we salvaged what we could of the equipment and moved on. The two damaged transports were ferried back to the Station for repair.

Once again the aliens had surprised us. They knew their own world far better than we did. But we were determined to press on, whatever the cost, because the alternative was the destruction of Earth and the end of our civilization. No quarter was expected and no quarter would be given. The Martians were defending their homes. We were defending our entire planet.

Only one of us would survive.

CHAPTER SIXTEEN
DOWN THE RABBIT HOLE

"Do you want to live forever?"
—Old military saying

ALEX SMITH, 23 BI-SEPTEMBER, MARS YEAR VII
NIER CRATER, PLANET MARS

The craggy walls of Nier Crater loomed deep and mighty above the Utopia Planitia plain like the fortification of some great medieval castle. We joined forces with Task Force II from the Granick Valley Station about a mile south of the perimeter, and General Burgess immediately ordered two patrols quickly to encircle the formation and report back. No obvious signs of life were found, other than the footprints of the great striders that had already been noted. There was also no clear entrance to the place, although some of the tripod tracks led to an area on one wall where there appeared to be some rough giant steps leading up to the rim and back down again on the other side.

The Martian weapons emplacement had been located on a rise in the exact center of the crater; this had been destroyed by one of our Warstations soon after we'd arrived in Mars orbit. The drones that we now placed over the crater still showed the site as devastated, but we knew that the aliens could be devious little creatures, and we trusted none of these observations.

The General ordered our forces to approach Nier from the south, spreading out from each flank as we did so. Our half-track, ZM-73, was commanded by Lieutenant McGoohan, and included ten noncoms in addition to myself. As we moved closer to the looming escarpment, suddenly I heard a loud clang on the front of our vehicle, and then another and another, like hail falling.

"What the fuck!" McGoohan said.

Bang-bang-bang-bang! I looked outside and saw small rocks bouncing along beside NX-01, one of the transports from Task Force II.

"I think they're shooting pellets at us," I said.

Then there was a huge ka-thump, and the ground shook with the force of the impact.

"Some of the rocks appear to be a little larger than others," Corporal Drake said laconically.

The bigger stones were being lofted from within the crater itself, but the smaller ones emanated from small apertures on the stone wall in front of us.

"Return fire!" General Burgess ordered, and we opened up with a broadside of cannons and lasers, interspersed with missiles.

From above, shafts of bright light shot down from one of our Warstations, quickly putting the largest of the Martian weapons out of commission.

"Withdraw!" came the order, and we did so in smart fashion.

When we reached the assembly area, we took stock of our situation. The transports were covered with dents, but had otherwise suffered relatively minor damage, except for a few broken lights, some bent communications gear, and similar annoyances. One of the battery trucks carrying the solar cell arrays, however, had had a number of its pieces shattered into oblivion. These obviously would have to remain behind during any future action.

A few members of the Advisory Council then joined Burgess in his command vehicle.

"What've we got?" he asked.

"Well, sir, we're still basically OK," Major Levine said,

"but we weren't able to knock out many of the smaller enemy weapons sites. They seem to be well embedded within the rock surface itself, to the point where you would have to tear apart the entire structure just to reach them. I have no idea how they're serviced or operated. Maybe there are tunnels of some kind in the wall of the crater.

"The problem as I see it is this: these pellet guns are certainly not capable of damaging our half-tracks to any great degree. We can operate with impunity pretty much anywhere out here. But as soon as we begin exiting our vehicles to assault the crater proper, they'll immediately become deadly to our soldiers. Our men have no way of protecting themselves against these things. The stones're traveling fast enough that they'll seriously injure or kill any individual who's hit by one."

The commander frowned.

"Do we know how these weapons are triggered?" When nobody replied, he said: "I thought not. Major, send one of our half-tracks closer to the crater. I want to monitor exactly when the pellet guns are activated."

Levine got on the horn to Lieutenant Kirk in NX-01, and then we watched on the viewscreen as the transport slowly moved towards Nier. The stones started raining down around his vehicle at about 126 yards. When he pulled his truck back to 127, they stopped.

"Looks like an automated system to me," Burgess said. "Now the question becomes, how big does the intruder have to be to trigger a response?"

So we tried a variety of larger and smaller targets, until we figured out that a slow-moving man crawling along the ground would not activate the Martian defense system. We also discovered that there was a "dead zone" in the area where the striders apparently had been climbing to the rim. So we used this particular region as a staging area for our own teams.

I went to General Burgess directly.

"Sir, I'd like to accompany Company Six"—the team from our half-track—"I realize that I'm not regular Army, but I think

I can help. I'll try not to get in the way."

"Smith, why do I have to listen to your shit when I'm in the middle of putting this operation together?" he asked.

Then he picked up the com and yelled "Get over here!" into it. I didn't know who was on the other end.

"You still lurking around?" he said to me a minute later. "Christ! Let it be on your head then. And God help your sorry ass if you get in the way of my men, or cause any of them to be killed or injured. Now, get out of my sight!"

He switched to another channel on the com.

"McGoohan," he ordered, "Smith has my permission to tag along with your company when you move out. Yeah, I know, it's six of one, half a dozen of another. Just do it!"

And that was how I managed to talk my way onto the first assault wave.

It took us several hours to grind our noses through the dust and rocks up to the face of the huge crater. We took no chances, basically crawling the entire way. Each of the so-called "steps" reaching up the side of the flank was about twenty feet high. They appeared to have been deliberately cut into the stone a very long time ago indeed, probably tens of millions of years or longer, and had worn considerably in the interim. Some of the platforms had almost crumbled in subsequent rock falls, or appeared to be in danger of collapse. Our special ops teams had to scale each face from scratch, and then set up cords and pulleys to allow the rest of our troops to follow them.

For the first time I had some sense of the antiquity of the Martian civilization. How much might these creatures know, how much might they have learned over the eons? What could they tell us, if only we could find a way to communicate with them like civilized beings? What secrets of the cosmos could they reveal? Were there others out there like them?

I was confident that the aliens would know the answer to at least the final question. If they'd developed space travel by the end of the era of the dinosaurs, sixty-five million years ago, they could very well have spanned part of the galaxy itself. Time means very little to a culture that has so much of it to waste. This is a luxury that humanity has always lacked.

Were my dreams a form of communication, or were they just my own weird imaginations, the workings of my inner soul, the result of the trauma that I had suffered during the original War of Two Worlds? I had no idea. I felt that the Martians were close, very close now, to where we were standing, but it was only a vague sense, a "touch," if you will—and none of it, of course, none of it was verifiable.

I think one of our people counted ninety-six steps up the face of that damnable rock wall. It took us the better part of two days to make the ascent. It was bitterly cold and windy and unbeliev-ably nasty up there on the side of that unprotected expanse, and the protective suits we carried didn't help matters any. Some of the rock faces had sharp edges, and at least two Marines died when their environmental coverings ripped.

The aliens, however, had fallen silent again; we were not challenged in the slightest when we were at our most vulner-able.

Around noon on the third day we reached the top, which was actually a fairly broad and level area that showed signs of the passage of the striders. In the distance across the gap we could spy the far side of the crater. Down below, other than the destruction of the central peak, there was nothing to be seen except a shadowed depression off to one side. We quickly deter-mined that the fighting-machine tracks ended at the edge of that pit, if that's what it was. Our spy drones could not see much of anything in the declivity due to the way the shadows were positioned there.

It only took us another day to find our way down the inner flank of the crater. We performed a few tests to make certain that the Martians hadn't posted pellet guns on the interior walls of Nier, but there was no response. Obviously, the alien weapons were an external defensive system only.

We again came back to the same question as before: where were the Martians? And the only logical answer seemed to point towards the shallow, shadowy pit.

We set up camp near its rim, and carefully dispatched patrols throughout the floor of the crater. Since all of our men had to operate on foot, this took several days of careful peering and probing and prodding. There was nothing but burnt wreckage to mark the central peak of the structure; indeed, much of the hill had been blasted away by bombardment from our orbital Warstations. We found very little else to salvage, mostly unidentifiable pieces of scrap metal.

The pit itself, however, was much more interesting: it was actually a carefully maintained, broad earthen ramp that wound its spiral way down into the bowels of the planet. We had no probes that were really appropriate for exploring this kind of structure. It would have to be accomplished on foot. We all knew what we had to do.

That evening I discovered that Reverend Lesley was part of our mission, having ridden in with Task Force II. She was going around the camp, offering "comfort to the troops" prior to our assault of the Martian facility on the next day.

"Place your trust in God," she said through her mask (I recognized the thin, whiny voice immediately), "for He never lets you down."

When she spotted me, she pretended like she didn't know me, although I saw the jolt of recognition flicker over her body. I thought the Martians had drained her of her blood back on Earth, after she'd been trapped with me for two terrible weeks in the awful house in Marin County.

She kept her distance, but inevitably our two orbits intersected when we picked up our MREs.

"Excuse me," she said.

"Well, Reverend," I said, "I see that you were saved after all."

"God heard my prayers, and he defeated the Martians before they could abuse me. My faith remains yet intact."

"Whatever happened to your parish, St. Gandalf's Church in San Rafael?"

"Oh, that was a long time ago, that was a very long, uh, it was awhile back. I found my calling elsewhere, Dr. Smith. I wanted to see the devil-spawn destroyed by the hand of Almighty God. I wanted to see them dead and condemned to everlasting fire in the eternal pits of hell."

"Do you dream, Reverend Lesley?"

"Dream! No, no, I never dream!" she said, rattling off the words, rat-a-tat-tat. "Why would you think such a thing? I never, ever stray from the word of God."

"Really? So you don't have visions of the great salt pools with their caressing weed?"

"No!" she almost shouted. "I don't see anything. Really! I never dream! I am utterly steadfast in the sight of the Lord. He protects me from the aliens."

Then she grabbed her ration box and ran away.

"A little high-strung, isn't she?" Mayer said behind me.

"Just a little," I said. "Another wandering refugee from the War of Two Worlds."

"So where are we going tomorrow?"

"Down the ole rabbit hole, down to Wonderland itself."

"Ha, ha, ha," he said. "Maybe we'll see Alice."

"Or the White Rabbit. We could see a whole goddam menagerie down there."

CHAPTER SEVENTEEN
FIFTY FATHOMS DEEP

Half owre, half owre to Aberdour,
'Tis fifty fathoms deep;
And there lies gude Sir Patrick Spens,
Wi' the Scots lords at his feet!
—Old Ballad

ALEX SMITH, 1 BI-OCTOBER, MARS YEAR VII
BENEATH NIER CRATER, PLANET MARS

But before we could descend into the depths of Mars, we had to prepare battery-powered carts to tote our weapons and supplies, with lights to help show the way. These were airlifted by shuttle from both the Isis and Granick Valley Stations. I hoped that the alien ramp would extend downward for at least part of the journey. The Martians had no evident concept of the wheel—at least we'd seen none thus far—and so one might expect that their "roads," if they even regarded them that way, would be rough and filled with steps and drops instead of gradual declines. Why this particular structure was different from the rest was beyond me. It just reflected our basic ignorance of this alien civilization.

Our scientists also took careful measurements of the air rising out of the pit, and then presented their findings to the Council, which was again linked through videoconferencing back to our bases, both planet-side and on the moons Deimos and Phobos.

"There's evidence of some warmth, moisture, and oxygen," they said, "although we won't know the full extent of the atmosphere until we reach bottom. We did expect to find something like this, given the ability of the Martians to adapt even roughly to the environmental conditions on Earth."

But the analysis told us very little else, beyond revealing an array of trace elements that seemed to correspond with the known physiology of Martian life in general.

"Oh," one of them—I think it was Dr. Scott—said almost as an afterthought, "we also found what appears to be pollen from the red weed."

We tried dangling auditory sensors as far as we could reach into the entranceway of the hole, but beyond a faint, regular thumping sound, they recorded nothing. The noise, when I heard it played back, reminded me of the racket generated by the digging-machine that I witnessed in the Martian pit on Earth.

We employed seismometers as well, plus a bunch of other equipment that I can't even describe and whose names I don't know, but they told us nothing new. We just had to go down there to see for ourselves.

For some strange reason, though, even the General was hesitant about making the first move. This was a man who was known for his decisiveness, for his ability to make quick judgments, but there's something daunting about entering upon a wholly alien universe. This is the way the world ends, not with a bang, but a whimper. Still, it had to be done, and the sooner, the better, as we all knew.

And so on the first day of the new month we started on our long journey to the center of the world.

The light faded very quickly as we headed ever downwards, gradually leaving us in a persistent gloom that we could barely penetrate, even with our lanterns at full intensity. I kept my left hand pressed against one of the rock walls to help steady myself, but paused a moment when I detected a subtle change in the surface. I turned, stepped backwards slightly, and flashed my lamp over the thing.

"My God," I said. "Look at this!"

More lights were brought into play to illuminate the entire wall, as members of our group gathered around behind me, pushing to see what I'd discovered. Cut into the stone facing was a framed picture inlaid with minerals and different-colored rocks. It depicted what was obviously a Martian alien, although perhaps a more primitive version of the creature (it had a smaller head), lying partly in and out of the water along an ancient shoreline. Small red plants (or possibly animals) of an unknown species lay further up the beach.

"It's beautiful!" Lieutenant Verne said, and so it was, completely unlike anything that I'd ever seen on Earth.

We moved on to the second *tableau*, and this displayed the same Martian, but now completely freed from the imprisoning waves. And so it continued, frame after frame, showing the development of the alien civilization during some distant, dim past of the Red Planet.

The use of visual contrast, the brightness of the colors, the choice of minerals that sparkled and changed under different light, all worked together to create an impression of something vivid and almost moving on that cold stone wall. This was Mars as the Martians saw it. For the first time, I thought, we could envision them as something different than just soulless killers.

We saw the great hives of the aliens, we watched as the oceans gradually receded and finally dried up completely, we viewed the huge excavations that preserved whatever could be saved of the creatures' habitat, we envisioned the coming of other visitors from outer space and the community of the stars, we experienced the development of Martian space travel, we noted with alarm the arrival of the dinosaur-men from Earth and their attacks on the Martian pits, we gasped when the great meteor was moved from its orbit and nudged towards its final impact with Earth, we cried when our homeworld was almost destroyed, and again when we realized how little had been left intact on Mars for the aliens to maintain.

These were creatures who obviously felt very deeply. These

were intelligent beings who had struggled to live peacefully within their own world for hundreds of millions or even billions of years, and had only fought back to prevent their own passing.

The artwork that we saw, although utterly alien in its conception and its execution, was of such a high order as to take our breaths away. How had it come to this trial of "Us vs. Them"? Why did we have to kill each other? Was there not some other way? Could we not all just get along?

All of us, I think, pondered these revelations during that long passage down through the spiral way. And how could we not? There must be some method of communicating with the Martians. There had to be. Destroying them would be an excuse, not a resolution of the conflict.

Down and down and down we drove, reaching into the very bowels of the Red Planet, uncovering more and more of the past of this strange world, unraveling more and more of the mystery of the aliens.

Where were the Martians?

Why, they were evident all around us. They were embedded in these mosaics, each and every one. You could see them peering out from the panoplies, their eyes glittering with the minerals that the ancient artist had used to depict their intelligence. Only the aliens showed those sparkling eyes.

Around and 'round and 'round the road ran, creeping ever further into the heart of the world, and as we went on, the atmosphere changed and the temperature warmed, until one of the scientists, Dr. Scott, looked at several of his instruments and suddenly removed his mask. He took a deep breath and then exhaled.

"Amazing," he said, coughing before carefully removing and stowing his gloves. "According to my readings, it's perfectly safe: a little musty, perhaps, but quite, uh, quite passable."

One by one we followed suit. The air temperature, according to our instruments, was about forty degrees Fahrenheit. The oxygen content of the atmosphere here was very close to that of Earth, although the thin pressure was equivalent to that of a high mountain. We had to be careful of over-exertion.

"How do they keep the air from seeping out?" someone asked.

"I dunno," Scott said, "but obviously they do."

I could see my breath as I blew it out my mouth.

By now everyone had removed their breathers.

"Stow them," General Burgess ordered. "We'll take a break here."

Throughout the four-hour period that we'd been gradually descending into the Martian pit, we had heard nothing but the creaking of the carts and the stomping of our own boots upon the loose Earth. We could still see signs of the imprints of the great pads of the striders upon the road in front of us, although how the fighting-machines could fit within the fifteen-foot ceilings was unknown. I remembered then the tripod that had been stationed by the pit guarding the house in which I'd been trapped in California some dozen years before, and how it had telescoped down upon itself when not in operation—and I mentioned this to the General and to Dr. Scott as we squatted in the dirt and munched on our MREs.

I burped and swigged a sip of water, and then put my box aside.

"Do you want those?" Mayer suddenly asked, appearing beside me and pointing down at my leftovers.

"I've had quite enough, thanks," I said. "You can have the rest if you really want them."

"I do, I do!" he said, and wolfed down the tasteless orts with obvious relish, although no relish was evident to my eyes.

Some contractor had made a fortune developing this crusty crapola, I thought to myself, but not one of those damned indus-trialists had ever actually eaten any of it! The one thing that I deeply regretted about leaving Earth was the abandonment of any future prospect of a decent meal. Maybe the hydro-ponics lab at the base would provide a variety of produce in the future—we certainly hoped so—but the sauces, the spices, the fresh meat, the eggs and milk and cheese (no vegetarian here,

I'm afraid!), the newly baked bread, the truly distinctive dining experience, all of that was gone for good.

C'est la vie! C'est la guerre!

Half an hour later we were back on our feet again, once more heading towards the Gates of Hell. "Abandon hope all ye who enter here!"

Fifty fathoms deep we delved, fifty fathoms and more; we probed and quested and roamed the deep, but never found the shore.

We never did find Sir Patrick Spens and the Scots lords, either.

CHAPTER EIGHTEEN
GO DOWN AGAIN TO THE DEPTHS

They mount up to the heaven,
They go down again to the depths.
—Bible, *Psalms 107:26*

ALEX SMITH, 2 BI-OCTOBER, MARS YEAR VII
BENEATH NIER CRATER, PLANET MARS

It took us four more hours to hit bottom. We came around a bend in the spiral road descending into the great Martian pit, and suddenly exited into a grand ballroom of the depths.

The place was so vast, so looming in its immensity that our lights couldn't penetrate the swirling mists to reach any of the walls on the far side of the chamber, wherever that was. We gathered together just outside the entranceway to take stock.

"We'll set up base camp here," General Burgess said. "Major Levine, establish the usual defensive perimeter. Captain Clarke, we'll serve the evening meal before proceeding any further...."

And so on. We had a number of airtight tents with us, but not enough to house several hundred troops, so most of the soldiers had to hunker down in the open on the bare soil of the cave floor. While all of these things were in preparation, I and several others took the opportunity to scan the nearby walls.

"More pictures," Alan Scott said, flashing his light up onto the facing. "And what's this?"

He'd found another opening in the rock, this one much

smaller than the fifteen-foot-high and –wide road that we'd traveled to reach this place. Its diameter was about five feet in all directions, and it was set a foot or two off the dirt floor.

Then Dr. Eugene Markus spotted another and I found a third, and soon we were all shouting about the holes peppering the nearby chamber walls. Some were right down towards the surface of the pit, like our original entranceway, but others reached halfway or more up the hundred-foot expanse. There seemed to be no pattern to them.

I went up close to the one that I'd discovered, and flashed my light inside. It curved off into the indecipherable distance to the right, its bare rock structure giving no hint whatever at its utility.

Then we were called to supper. Several noncoms had been ordered to prepare a hot meal, a kind of stew fashioned from several special food packets that had been included on our mission, together with some faintly warm cornbread; and the combination, after several days of our eating tasteless tripe, did wonders for our morale.

Afterwards, General Burgess called a meeting of our Advisory Council, but we soon realized that we'd lost contact with the surface.

"We had communication during our lunch break," one of the officers said.

"Send a two-man patrol back up the ramp to re-establish a radio link," the commander ordered.

"Yes, sir."

We had just sat down on the dirt floor of the cave to discuss our options for the following day, when the com came alive again.

Lieutenant Tim Edwards took the call, and then turned to the General, holding one hand over the mouthpiece.

"Sir," he said. "The exit is blocked."

"What!" Burgess said. "Let me talk to them."

He mumbled into the mike for a moment, yelled "Shit!" once, and then ordered the men on the other end of the line to "Remain where you are until further notice!"

"About a quarter mile up the ramp," he said to our group, "a large sheet of metal has now sealed the passageway. They think it descended from the ceiling."

"Can we blow the door, sir?" Levine asked.

"I don't know, but I want you to find out. The danger if we try anything is that we might be able to dislodge the plating all right, but in the process we could bring down the tunnel itself, thereby trapping us down here. Try to determine how thick the metal is and what it consists of, plus the composition of the rock facing.

"In the meantime, I want to begin surveying this cavern as soon as the men've had a chance to rest, beginning at 0600 tomorrow morning. We'll run patrols along the walls until they make contact with each other on the opposite side. Have them check in with command every five minutes. I also want a squad sent straight out into the middle of the chamber. Finally, dispatch a survey party a few hundred yards into one of these side tunnels. Let's see what's in there."

"Yes, sir," the junior officers all said in unison.

For the moment, however, everyone settled down to make our temporary camp as comfortable as possible. The lighting was reduced to just the picket line to conserve power. The men talked among themselves for awhile, and then several of them played the small electric mouth organs that had become so popular in recent years; but the overall atmosphere seemed subdued. We were all waiting for something to happen, and we didn't quite know what. Gradually, the soldiers gave up any attempt at conversation, and went to sleep, one by one. The darkness and humidity was almost oppressive, even though the temperature couldn't have been more than sixty or seventy. Only the small glows emanating from the guard stations provided a distant comfort.

The "music" began sometime after midnight. I was deep asleep by then, and in my dreams I was conversing with the Martians and they were talking back.

"You see how it is, my dear Dr. Smith," one of them was saying, speaking like an English toff, "We are so very few down here and you are so many, and all we want is for you to share some of your vital fluids with us. Is that so hard, truly?"

"But I can't spare anything, truly I can't," I cried out. "You know the score: better dead than red!"

"Really, old chap," another one of the aliens said, a bowler hat set at a jaunty angle on its domed head, "is that actually cricket? After all, we ask so very, very little of you. I mean, we rather have you at our mercy, so to speak—nudge, nudge, wink, wink, and all that. Just give us a bitty, tasty, fruity sip of the nip, and you can go home again."

"But, but, you can't go home again!"

Then it pulled out a phone fashioned somehow out of the red weed, and held it to the back of its head, where its single ear was located. A writhing thread of the weed trailed from the end of the thing off into the distance. It shook the instrument a few times.

"Bad connection," it said, before holding the phone in front of it with one of its tentacles and shaking the thing again. The phone squawked an *"Oh-lah, hoo-lah-lah."*

"Ah," the alien said. Then it held the instrument in front of its face and began speaking into it quite loudly: "Wonderland Wax Museum, Marmaduke Q. Martian speaking. Time to send in the bodacious bunny, what! Signing off: *ooh-lah, ooh-lah!*"

The White Rabbit suddenly appeared on the scene, and I knew we weren't in Kansas anymore. The albino Lepus promptly pulled a flute from his back "pouch," and began playing a haunting air that I didn't recognize. About that time the stirring of my fellow explorers nudged me awake.

"What *is* that?" they were whispering back and forth to each other.

I sat up, throwing off my thin cover. Somewhere, every-where, a faint whistling was filling the expanse.

"It's got to be the air rushing through the tunnels," someone said.

"Right," someone else added.

But slowly the sound began to grow and change, waxing and waning seemingly without pattern, interspersed with the hooting and hollering that we'd associated with the Martians back on Earth; and it filled the space with its echoes and reverberations, rolling back and forth, to and fro, as if some mad organist was practicing an *outré* version of Johann Sebastian Bach's *Brandenburg Concertos*. I find it now nearly impossible to express the utter strangeness of it all.

My fellow sufferers reacted in different ways. A few never even woke, or so they claimed, although how anyone could have slept through all that racket is beyond me. Several started yelling or screaming their frustration to the four winds. One man pulled out a gun and began shooting his weapon into the distant darkness, until he was subdued by his comrades-in-arms. And several, myself included, wept.

As alien as the music was, it touched us all somehow, albeit in different ways. For me, it reached deep inside my soul and wrapped itself around the memories of my experiences of the War of Two Worlds, and intertwined them with what I was feeling now. I cried for the gap in understanding between our species, a chasm that I knew not how to bridge.

"Vanity of vanities, saith the Preacher, vanity of vanities, all is vanity. What profit hath a man of all his labor which he taketh under the sun?"

Suddenly I rose to my feet, and stepping over and around my fellow men, walked away into the darkness towards the center of the cavern. I know not even to this day what impulse guided me, or how I avoided whatever pitfalls there might have been around me. Somehow the music lured me on. Somehow I had to go. I had to bear witness. Something was calling me, *had* been calling me for nigh onto thirteen years.

I placed one foot in front of another, and padded my way out into the center of that great room, listening to the music of the spheres, looking for I knew not what.

I walked the straight path for a very long time, and then I

came to a pool of open water, a pond of cool, almost chilly fluid percolating upwards from somewhere down below. I fell to my knees, bent my tired face down to its sparkling surface, and drank deeply of the bubbly liquid.

"Give strong drink unto him that is ready to perish, and wine unto those that be of heavy hearts. Let him drink, and forget his poverty, and remember his misery no more."

And I lived.

CHAPTER NINETEEN
I SING THE BODY ELECTRIC

The contract 'twixt Hannah, God, and me,
Was not for one or twenty years, but for eternity.
—Petroleum V. Nasby

ALEX SMITH, 3 BI-OCTOBER, MARS YEAR VII
BENEATH NIER CRATER, PLANET MARS

They found me lying unconscious beside the drying, mud-caked remains of a damp area in the soil. When roll call was taken at 0400 (everyone having been stirred awake either by the incessant noise or by their fellow voyagers), a half dozen members of the expedition failed to respond. Further checking revealed the footprints of the wanderers heading off in different directions from the camp. One had crawled into one of the smaller tunnels in the wall, another had followed the edge of the cave in one direction, and so on. Each was tracked down individually, but not all were found. Two went missing completely.

I was brought the half mile back to our encampment and revived. I could remember everything up to my drinking the water from the pond, but nothing thereafter. I'd been missing for at least eight hours by the time they located me.

Then began the grilling. General Burgess and the scientists and the doctors and the other military men all wanted to know what I recalled of the previous night—which was not much. The same questions were asked over and over again. I think they regarded me as tainted somehow by my experience, or at least very suspect.

"You have to look at it from our point of view, Smith," Dr. Stephen Andrews said. "You go walking off into nowhere by yourself, you have no explanation as to why or how or what prompted you, and no memory of what occurred after a certain point. You remember talking with Martians who weren't actually there (by your own admission), and drinking from a pool that doesn't exist any longer."

"But you found traces of the water," I said.

"Yes, we did find traces, which are more than we've located anywhere else on this planet to date. The soil was still damp, and our preliminary analyses, with what few instruments we have available to us down here, indicate that the stuff was potable. But you have to admit that it's damned strange, all of it."

I acknowledged such with a sudden humility that I was unused to experiencing. I had no idea of what had happened or was happening to me.

"Anyway, Burgess wants you kept under constant observation for the rest of this mission. You're not to be left alone. Also, I want to check your vitals every few hours. If you *did* drink some Martian water, we have to make certain that you haven't picked up some alien bug in the process."

The music had ceased before I'd been found, as abruptly as it had started. Throughout the day, that very hectic day, the General had gone forward with his plans to thoroughly survey the chamber. Patrols had been dispatched in all directions.

As a consequence, we now knew that the other side of the cavern was about 1.67 miles distant; there was another major exit tunnel, of a size and shape similar to the one by which we had entered the cave, exactly opposite to our own. The width of the expanse was approximately 2.31 miles. Its height at the periphery was about a hundred feet, but the dome increased to almost two hundred feet in the center.

On the left-hand side of the space we made a very interesting discovery. Lined up on the open floor, in row upon row, were the Martian fighting-machines, empty and desolate, their legs collapsed down to their resting postures, which left them about fifteen feet off the ground, their cabs empty, and in many cases their general status obviously inoperative. Some showed quite evident signs of advanced age and decay and disrepair. There were no tracks of the aliens themselves.

"What do we do with these things?" Major Levine asked.

"Nothing," was the final judgment.

This appeared to be the equivalent of nothing more than a Martian junkyard.

So where were the Martians?

In all the time since we'd landed our expedition, we had only actually seen one of the creatures fleeing from its downed strider, and we hadn't been able to capture or kill that particular individual. Everything else consisted of mere dreams and phantoms. I was beginning to wonder how many of the aliens were actually left alive. The Red Planet was so desiccated, so lacking in basic amenities, that it surely could not support very many species or members of *any* species. If the Martians were at the top of their food chain, as we were of ours, then they must have dwindled down to a very few survivors indeed.

The rump Advisory Council met again that evening, and we debated furiously over what we should now do.

"We have to press on," I said. "We can't go back, since the Martians have sealed the only known exit point. We've barely begun to explore this nest, if that's what it is, and we need to know more, much more, if we're going to find any workable strategy to defeat the aliens."

In the end, no one had any better argument, save Reverend Lesley, bless her mercenary soul, who began ranting again about the devilish nature of the enemy, and how God had condemned them to the eternal depths—quite literally—and that we should have nothing to do with them, lest we be tainted ourselves and sent straight to Hell.

Overall, her ravings were not well received, but what troubled me is that I could see a few heads nodding amongst the ordinary soldiers. The longer we were stuck down here in this pit, the greater the possibility that the irrational would somehow become plausible. Desperate people will resort to desperate means to end their despair.

We determined finally to dismantle our camp the next day, and proceed through the major tunnel on the other side of the chamber.

That night the Martian music returned, with its oohing and ahing and whistling, and we got very little sleep as a result. I dreaded the thought of experiencing more of the surrealistic dreams, which I couldn't control and which always left me profoundly disturbed afterwards. What few naps I managed to take, however, failed to elicit quite the same response in my psyche. My sleep was undisturbed save for the howling racket that wrenched at us all.

I was utterly weary the next day, and I wondered whether this aural display had been put on especially by the Martians just for our benefit, or if this was something that played on and on throughout the night on a constant basis, irrespective of the audience. I had no answer then, and I have none now. Perhaps it was just the alien equivalent of Muzak.

That morning we packed everything up and set out again, first crossing the cavern, and then entering the passage on the other side. It had very similar dimensions to the tunnel from the surface, including a flat, dirt floor, smoothly polished stone walls, and mosaic murals posted at discrete intervals. Each of the pieces of alien artwork was different from the previous ones; we never saw one that was exactly the same as any other. That the Martians were a supremely artistic race was now a given.

But other than the pictures, we found nothing else: no signs of life, no furniture, no weapons, no artifacts, no machines, nothing.

Where were the Martians?

That day we traveled at least ten miles into the bowels of the Red Planet. Our passageway was straight as an arrow. We frequently encountered side tunnels of various sizes, but all were empty and stark, so far as we could determine. Our scientists sometimes detected faint breezes blowing in or out of these openings, and occasionally we smelled an odor of, well, something unusual but indefinable. These traces could be either pleasant or unpleasant to the senses, and sometimes both to different individuals at the same time.

By late afternoon we were beginning to look for someplace suitable to make camp again.

"What's that?" PFC Mayer said.

He was then sharing the point position of our column. We all stopped, straining to peer into the impenetrable darkness. Very far away I could barely detect the "thump, thump, thump" of some mighty engine at work.

We pressed forward as quickly as we dared, hoping against hope that the sound of the machine represented some sign of the great Martian civilization that we had all been expecting to find.

The general noise level increased substantially as we continued to march down that endless corridor in stone. We noticed that the mosaics were also altering with time, gradually becoming focused on the development of alien science and technology. Our excitement grew as we came closer to the site.

Suddenly another huge cavern opened wide before us. We shined our lights as far into the space as possible, but could only make out the shadows of some immensely looming monstrosities. Then a great spark of electricity spanned the gap between two of the structures, giving us the glimpse of an absolutely enormous complex of interconnected machinery. I spied the arm of a hundred-foot piston churning its way back and forth, like the leg of some giant grasshopper, doing its job with a doggedness and determination that seemed utterly inhuman. But nowhere did we find any evidence of controllers or operators.

What the great machines were actually accomplishing here remained a mystery to us. Dr. Scott thought that it had something to do with the circulation of the atmosphere, pointing specifically to the large, round, flexible tubing that seemed to connect the apparatus to the walls and ceiling of the cavern. But this was only a guess, as even he would have readily admitted. The equipment could just as easily have been circulating water or something else of vital need to the aliens. We dared not touch anything lest the resulting interruption rebound upon us in some fatal way. We just documented meticulously whatever we could with photographs, hoping that someone somewhere would be able to figure out what was happening here.

It was now mid-evening, and all the men were hungry and tired. The racket in the cavern, however, was so great that we couldn't possibly have camped in one of the open spaces there, so we retreated back along the main corridor a mile or two until we found an area near a cross junction where the noise level was bearable. Then we settled down for a cold meal and incessant conversation about what we'd just observed.

"Not like Nob Hill," Mayer said, hunkering along me. "Now *that* was something special!"

"Yeah." I was trying to masticate some of the mushy mess that passed for food in our kits. "The wine was good there."

"Nothing like that here!"

I finally gave him the rest of my rations, which is obviously what he was looking for.

"I'm going to sleep." I was dead-tired from our exertions and from the lack of rest during the previous two nights.

I had no trouble finding Dreamland again, but whatever I saw there, I failed to remember afterwards.

About three the next morning, there was a whoosh of air and sound nearby that washed right over us, crashing one of the tents in upon itself, and rapidly receding off into the distance.

"What the fuck was that!" Mayer said.

The guards, who'd mostly been dozing themselves, came to attention, pointing their guns into the deep recesses of the dark.

"What's going on?" Burgess asked.

"I dunno, sir," one of the sentinels said. "Something went right by us, I think, in that other tunnel."

The cross corridor was about fifteen feet away. We crowded out into the junction of the two passageways, but saw nothing, either in the distance as far as we could see down the side channels, or on the dirt surface of the connecting roads. We looked and looked, but found no evidence of what had just swooshed by.

Then the Martian music began again.

"I sing the body electric," I said.

No one answered me.

They were all scared half to death.

CHAPTER TWENTY
ZEPHYR AND BOREAS

Everybody talks about the weather,
but nobody does anything about it.
—Charles Dudley Warner

ALEX SMITH, 4 BI-OCTOBER, MARS YEAR VII
BENEATH NIER CRATER, PLANET MARS

"There was definitely something there?" General Burgess asked.

"Well, I think so, sir," the noncom said. "It's just that it all happened so fast, and we really couldn't see anything, it was too far away. I couldn't even tell you which way it was going."

The officer ran his hand back through his thinning gray hair. He looked ten years older than the day he'd landed at Isis Station. He gazed around at the dozen *ad hoc* members of the Advisory Council present on our expedition.

"Ideas, anyone?" he asked.

We were gathered in a semi-circle around the commander's tent at our makeshift campsite. We all glanced at each other and shook our heads.

"Come on, people. We started with enough supplies to last just two weeks down here. We're already into our fourth day, and we have no more answers than before. The main exit's blocked, and communications have been cut."

"We follow the whatever-it-was," I said.

"But which way?"

"Both ways, sir. We have no choice."

Everyone began nodding in agreement.

"Damn. I don't really like the idea of splitting our forces, I really don't. Lieutenant McGoohan and Lieutenant Kirk, you'll take your respective companies together with at least one each of the scientists and anyone else you think necessary or appropriate, and you'll proceed right and left up the corridors. I'll remain here with the main expedition, while the rest of our crew investigates the machine room. Check in every fifteen minutes, gentlemen."

In the end, McGoohan picked me and Mayer and, for whatever reason, Reverend Lesley, in addition to the ten members of Company Six, plus Dr. Markus, the exobiologist. We moved out at 0700, heading in what appeared to be a northerly direction. Kirk and his men turned south.

The cross passage had dimensions very similar to those of the main corridor that we'd been traversing, being perhaps slightly smaller in diameter, and lacking the wall mosaics that decorated the other. I could feel a slight breeze blowing against my face; it gave off a fragrance of things growing, the smell of grass and brush and similar kinds of plants. The wind seemed to me gradually to increase as we walked forward, just slightly enough to be noticeable.

We stopped after five miles to rest and have lunch, breaking out the not-so-delicious MREs.

"Anyone want tooty-fruity?" Mayer asked.

"You're kidding, right?" Rogers said.

"That's what it says."

"A new low for the Armed Forces of the United States," I spoke in a deliberately sepulchral voice.

"Anyone notice something different about this tunnel?" Gene Markus asked.

"No girlie pictures?" Mayer said.

"That's disgusting." Reverend Lesley made a face.

Mayer stuck his tongue out at her and she grimaced in return.

I thought we might have to send both of them to their respective corners.

"No, we haven't encountered any side-passages," Markus said.

"You're right," I said. "And the air pressure here seems much more insistent."

"Yeah, and there's that odor, too," Mayer said. "Stinks to high heaven, like something died down here."

"You just didn't use your deodorant this morning," Cassell said.

Then I heard something like the whining of a mosquito, a thin, very high-pitched sound somewhere off in the distance, gradually changing modulation. It took me a second to realize what it was.

"Up against the walls, quick," I yelled, grabbing my pack and pulling it to one side.

I flattened myself as tightly as I could back against the cold rock facing. The rest followed suit, but Cassell was a little too slow. Suddenly the whining noise revved rapidly up the scale, and there was this immense "splat," like a great bug hitting the windshield of a car traveling seventy miles an hour. The thing, whatever it was, didn't even slow down. It was gone in an instant. All I had was the impression before it hit Cassell of a great round dome and a brief sheen of glistening metal, so typical of a Martian bio-machine.

We were all splattered with blood and guts. The soldier had been pulverized by the impact: the only pieces of him that were still intact were his feet.

"Jesus, Jesus, Jesus, Jesus, Jesus!" Rogers was whimpering against the tunnel wall. "What *was* it?"

"Get a grip on yourself," the Lieutenant said.

He was meticulously wiping Cassell's vital fluids off his uniform. Lesley suddenly threw up to one side.

"We need to find some shelter here," I said.

"Agreed."

The officer spoke into the com and reported the situation.

Then he turned back to us grim-faced.

"Half of Company Twenty-Seven was lost. They're turning back. The main camp had two sentries killed at the junction. Nobody knew what it was until the thing was upon them."

"What about us, sir?" Rogers asked.

"It's up to me, and I've decided to move forward. Clean up as best you can, and let's get going, men."

"But, sir...."

"You heard my order," the Lieutenant said. "Move it!"

About mid-afternoon we reached a split in the highway, for that's obviously what this was, at least to my reckoning (no one else agreed with me, however). There was a "Y" in the tunnel, with one branch heading northeast (or whatever) and one north by northwest. The breeze blew more strongly from the eastern branch.

"Recommendations, anyone?" McGoohan asked.

Markus thought we ought to take the right-hand route, since the wind there was blowing towards us a little more forcefully. I suggested the opposite passageway. It was a case of Zephyr or Boreas, a Hobson's choice if I ever saw one. We offered our steeds no better options than Thomas Hobson ever did, and had as much basis on which to choose. So in the end we let chance decide, and as usual with these things, I was the luckiest man alive.

I should've kept my big mouth shut.

Up to this point the tunnels that we'd explored had all been arrow straight, save for the primary entrance hole from the planet's surface, the junctions with the other passages, and the "Y" we'd just encountered. Now, however, we began to notice a difference. This new road turned downward and to the left in a long, slow curve. The further we traveled, the warmer and moister it became, until we were all sweating with the effort. I think we were tempted to strip off some of our clothing, but we didn't want to lose our precious supplies, so we left things as they were.

We broke briefly for an evening meal about six o'clock, and

then started out again. Two hours later we came to a small chamber. It was completely empty. Lining the wall opposite us was a series of seven exits, all about five feet in diameter.

It was such an obvious place to camp that we put down our packs with some relief, without even being ordered to do so. Our feet were achy, some being spotted with blisters, and our shoulders hurt from lugging our heavy gear. We just collapsed where we stood, and did the minimum necessary to set up.

"Rogers, you'll take the first watch," the Lieutenant ordered, and we all groaned at the thought of having to get up throughout the night to do our hour-long stints.

I think I must have fallen asleep right after that, because I have no memory of anything that happened until the wee hours of the morning, when I was gruffly shaken awake by McGoohan, and told to take my place by the main entrance to the cavern. I broke open a small pouch of self-warming tea, and sipped on it while I tried to bring some energy to my eyelids.

I moved around a little to get the circulation flowing again, but in the process accidentally dropped my light. It cracked against the stone and went out. I was fiddling with the thing, attempting to get it working again, when I realized that I could see the seven tunnels of Cibola on the opposite wall. The cavern ceiling gave off a faint luminescence that none of us had noticed before. The glow was so intangible that any stronger source quickly overwhelmed it in the mind's eye. I stepped out into the corridor and saw that the same thing was true there. The pale light gave everything a kind of rosy hue.

"I'll be damned," I said. "This planet...."

Then the breeze came up again, gusting out of the seven smaller tunnels facing me, and I heard the faintest whisper of Martian song, but very different this time, low and soothing and somehow very satisfying, almost a lullaby of illumination; and then I noticed that the light above me was flickering in time with the music. The beauty of the scene made me gasp out loud, and charged into my soul with the bare intensity of its vision. Tears rolled down my cheeks. It was one of those rare occasions in life when an experience of sight or sound or perception gives one an epiphany of being.

I watched the Martian opera unfold for two full hours, until finally it faded away, just before my replacement stirred in his makeshift bed.

I knew then that they had done this thing only for me.

CHAPTER TWENTY-ONE
WAR AND PEACE

She always believed in the old adage,
"Leave them while you're looking good."
—Anita Loos

ALEX SMITH, 5 BI-OCTOBER, MARS YEAR VII
BENEATH NIER CRATER, PLANET MARS

I come now to the turning point of my narrative, and I do so with a heavy heart. God knows I tried, God knows I made every effort in both worlds, but it just wasn't enough, boys and girls. Maybe, as Reverend Lesley had said, maybe the Devil really *was* at work here. Or perhaps it was just bad luck, an ill wind, you might say, that wafted its black dust over all of us, and left us tainted by "sin"-sibility.

We had a choice the next day—we always had a choice—and the L.T. decided to go forward once again.

"Half a league, half a league, half a league onward, all in the valley of death rode the six hundred."

But to what end?—that was the question that we never asked ourselves.

We had seven possible roads open to us, so we opted for the middle way. The aperture was much smaller than any of the tunnels that we'd assayed previously, perhaps four or five feet in diameter, which meant that we could only pass through the entrance one by one. PFC Rogers took point, his weapon leading the charge. I was near the end of the line.

With my pack, I barely was able to squeeze into the hole, and the effort to crawl forward through the tight space left me breathless in very short order. I estimate that we advanced about a hundred yards before emerging by the side of a small pool.

This was the first real evidence of life that we'd found in the great Martian pit. Plants of different kinds grew in profusion up the walls of the chamber, spaced almost in a fashion that could be described as ornamental. The light was brighter here too, emanating from a special tile embedded in the center of the ceiling. Then I heard a splash, and one of the strange-looking, mammal-like bipeds emerged from the water, staring at us with its oversized eyes.

They looked very much like the classic depiction of the aliens that had supposedly landed at Roswell, New Mexico, in 1947: tall, spindly, with elongated hands and fingers, narrow faces, domed heads, and bulging bug eyes with large, expressive lids. Like their masters, they were uniformly gray in color, and hairless.

These were the creatures that had been included on the Martian spaceships in Year One to provide meals for the invaders. All had been drained of blood before arriving on Earth, and the only specimens we'd had to examine after the fact were fragmentary examples of their species.

Suddenly the thing opened its mouth and growled at us, revealing a set of small but very sharp and pointed teeth. I realized then that it was a wearing a belt and harness. It pulled out a stone knife and waved the weapon in our direction, advancing right at Rogers.

The soldier reacted without even thinking, shooting the creature in the chest with his rifle. The force of the slug blew the lightweight alien back into the water, staining the fluid red with its blood. A chittering sound filled the room, and then high screams of anger and sorrow as first one, and then another head poked its way out of the dozens of small holes lining the far wall. There must have been hundreds of the creatures living there, whole families of them, whatever those families actually constituted. We saw both younger and older examples of the species, although no obvious delineation of the sexes—this was typical of the Martian fauna.

Several of the monkey-creatures, for this is how we came to think of them, popped out of their lairs, drawing their weapons as they advanced, and Rogers mowed these down as well. What else could he do? McGoohan had completely lost control of the situation.

Then a small bolt of some kind shot out of a nest and bounced off the soldier's belt. More followed, and soon we were ducking and shooting, and then ducking some more. One of the little arrows struck Rogers's left hand. He quickly pulled it loose, and continued firing. Dozens of bodies were now piled on the beach on the opposite side of the pond.

"Damn, damn, damn!" Rogers was shouting.

I glanced over at him. He was shaking his hand and trying to squeeze his fingers, without much success. While he was massaging his arm, another bolt hit him, and then a third. He suddenly looked very puzzled, before toppling face first into the weedy pond.

The L.T. pulled him up on the near shore, turned him over, and then promptly gave up: the man was clearly dead. Then McGoohan himself was hit.

"Retreat!" he ordered. "Leave Rogers and leave me! Get out of here, all of you!"

He fired a burst at the nest openings, forcing the creatures back inside.

One by one, we popped into the exit tunnel and crawled the interminable distance back to the original chamber. The Lieutenant's firing ceased about the time I pulled myself out the other end. Half of us had left our packs behind in the pool room.

I heard PFC Brooker, the last of our troops in line, screaming for help halfway through the tunnel. Evidently, the creatures had caught up with him and were stabbing his legs with their knives. There was nothing we could do for the man. When his voice ceased hollering, Mayer rolled a grenade into the tunnel and blew it up.

"That'll stop 'em!" he said. "Let's get moving!"

But it *didn't* stop them. As we headed out the main exit, we could hear them talking to themselves—chitter, chitter, chitter—as they gathered for another attack. How many of them were there anyway?

The second time they came at us we mowed them down with our advanced weapons. They had no place to hide and no defense against bullets and explosives. But there were just so damned many of them.

We would fight them off, turn and run as far as we could down the passageway, turn again to meet the next charge, and so on, over and over. We killed hundreds of the bipeds, maybe more—and inevitably, they killed *us* one by one. We had to leave the bodies of our comrades behind. We salvaged what we could of their weapons and ammunition, which was now beginning to run short.

The professional soldiers were now all dead, except for Mayer; we were left with just him, Lesley, Markus, and myself out of our original complement. Mayer called for help on the com while we were running, and General Burgess immediately dispatched a rescue squad up the cross corridor—but it would take them hours and hours to reach us.

"We've got to do something," I said. "We're not going to make it otherwise."

"What?" Mayer coughed as we jogged along.

I was almost to the point of exhaustion myself. I knew that I wouldn't be able to continue this much longer.

"Do you have any explosives left?"

"Not much."

"Can you rig something quickly?"

"If I had a few moments—but there isn't enough time to set up."

"What if I give you the time?"

He glanced over at me strangely.

"You've about had it, haven't you?" he finally said.

"Yep."

"All right, then. Lesley and Markus," he ordered, "give Smith your rifles."

He had to pry the weapon out of the minister's cold, dead-like hands.

Then he turned to me: "Good luck, man. See you whenever."

The trio ran off 'round the bend, while I settled down with my weapons and waited for the monkey-creatures to appear. I thought of my wife and daughter then, and regretted that I wouldn't be able to say goodbye to them personally.

I could hear the alien bipeds approaching up the corridor, chittering at each other, occasionally screaming, and presumably hankering for my "blood." I sympathized: we'd no business killing off their kin. It had all been a terrible misunderstanding. Isn't it always?

I lay there patiently for them to come to me. After all, I had all the time in the world.

CHAPTER TWENTY-TWO
MONODY ON THE DEATH OF SHERIDAN

God will give him blood to drink!
—Nathaniel Hawthorne

ALEX SMITH, 5(?) BI-OCTOBER, MARS YEAR VII
BENEATH NIER CRATER, PLANET MARS

The pounding in my head was the incessant blat, blat, blat of the automatic rifles, as I mowed down the hordes of alien monkey-creatures charging at me up the tunnel. I brandished a weapon in each hand, and when the first had exhausted its ammunition, I replaced it with a third. Then I was down just to one, with several packs of ammo still remaining, and I knew the end was nigh.

They just wouldn't stop coming. I wish to God I'd known some way of communicating with the poor buggers, for whom I actually felt a certain amount of sorrow and shame, since it'd been our boys who'd started the whole business. If Rogers just hadn't shot that first one. But I couldn't speak "chitter," if indeed that was actually a language of sorts. I idly wondered as I was killing hundreds of the beasties whether or not they could really converse with each other. Talk about Alice in Wonderland!

But the end was nigh, as I said, and they knew it. I was down to my last clip plus the rounds in my pistol, one of which I intended for myself, when one of those damnable dart thingies struck me on my right arm. It was a chance shot, and I was surprised in a way that they hadn't nicked me before this. The evidence of their numerous attempts was littered all around my prone body.

It started as a tingling in my fingertips, then progressed to a kind of dull pain, and then…nothing. I lost all feeling in my right arm within minutes of being struck. I kept shooting with my left as best I could. I discarded my now-empty rifle, and with difficulty pulled out my pistol. I carefully shot them one at a time, counting mentally as I did so.

But before I could find surcease, my whole body just went limp, completely without warning. I knew that the poison had progressed from my arm into the rest of me.

The end was nigh.

I tried to whisper Becky's name, but all that emerged from my lips was a gurgle. I was still able to move my eyes, and I watched dispassionately as the monkey-creatures slowly approached my recumbent form, their knives raised high to carve me into shreds. I wondered if they ate meat. I had so much that I wanted to ask them, even then.

I waited for Death to greet me.

One of them, perhaps a leader (he wore a more elaborate sash), bent down towards my head and opened his mouth wide. I would have declined the offer if I'd had the strength; instead, I just watched as he unrolled a long tongue and licked the sweat and blood off my brow.

"Urúk!" he yelled. *"Urúk!"*

Then they gathered 'round, removed my pack, rolled me over on my back, and somehow lifted me up on their frail shoulders, a dozen or fifteen of them, and began toting me through a series of tunnels and passageways.

Things began to go gray about that time, and all I can recall of our journey was the endless flashing of light and dark lines on the ceiling, of which I had at times a very close view. Whenever we reached our destination, they placed me on a table, cut off my clothing, and washed me all over with some kind of oily fluid.

I lay there with everything hanging out, shivering with a reaction to the venom squirreling its way through my system, and knowing that I was going to die soon in some very unpleasant fashion. So I thought of the good times I'd had with Becky and Mellie, of how we'd laughed and loved and shared so much together, and I accounted myself lucky.

This room was much brighter than any other place that I'd yet encountered in the Martian underground. Again, the illumination seemed to emanate from some kind of special tile in the center of the ceiling. Since I could only look straight up, I couldn't make out clearly anything around me, only that the chamber was filled with machines and equipment of all kinds, looming just out of the edge of my vision. I could see lights pulsing on some of them, so the aliens obviously had electricity. I cursed my inability to view what was going on around me. I could barely hear the shuffling of the various critters nearby, but I had no idea what they were doing.

Something out of my sight grabbed my right arm and injected a fluid into it. My limbs were restrained with straps of some kind. Then the Martian appeared.

My first thought was that I had no idea that they grew so damned big. The specimens that we'd seen on Earth had been roughly four feet in both height and width. This one may have been seven feet or more in size. If the metal pallet on which I was lying was roughly three or four feet off the floor, which I think was about right, this creature loomed well over it.

It suddenly bent down and looked me in the eyes. I thought I was doomed right then and there, because I'd seen the feeding pattern of the Martians back on Earth. But it just gazed deeply into my soul, and then turned to what I realized was a companion on the opposite side of the table. Nothing verbal passed between them (I knew they were telepathic), but it grunted something at one of the biped attendants, and took from it an instrument of some kind.

For the next few hours it probed and prodded me, examining all of my orifices, taking samples (from what little I could observe) of my hair and skin and other things that I won't go into here. It was almost gentle in its manipulations of my body.

Then I saw the feeding-tube appear, and I was ready for the end. I breathed a prayer and said my goodbyes to my dear wife and daughter. I saw the probe extend out of my vision down towards my neck. I could feel nothing, of course, but a sense of euphoria slowly crept over me, a feeling of pleasure and lassitude and exhilaration. No wonder the monkey-things offered themselves to their masters! This was obviously their reward.

Then the Martian reared up again, withdrawing its blood-stained prong. It turned once more to its fellow creature, and they must have exchanged something between them, because they all abruptly left. The bipeds then appeared on either side of the pallet, lifted it up again, and took me to another room. There I was injected once more with something that I couldn't see, and gradually the feeling began returning to my arms and legs; and I knew that I would recover, at least for a little while longer. I needed to pee something fierce, but being strapped down as I was, I had no way of making known my needs to these creatures. Finally I just went, ashamed of both the odor and my lack of control. One of them promptly appeared to clean me up.

The temperature in this series of rooms was comfortable to my bare body, running perhaps in the mid-eighties. I could detect the light breeze of some ventilation system wafting over my skin as the feeling gradually returned. I had no way of telling how much time was passing or had passed. This could have been either Friday or Saturday, for all I knew.

An unknown interval later, one of the bipeds brought a tube to my lips, and prodded me to drink. I sipped some kind of sweetened liquid. It restored me wonderfully. Then I was given a few pieces of leaf on which to chew. I have no idea what plant the food derived from, but again, it seemed highly nourishing to me, and even a bit tasty. Then I slept for some hours.

I awoke while they were carrying me back into the laboratory, for that's what I assumed it was. My greeting party had now grown to a half dozen of the Martians, varying in size from the standard four-foot model to the "Big Guy," as I'd come to think of the seven-footer.

"Howdy-do!" I said, now that I had my voice back.

They all looked at me suddenly very strangely. I'm not sure whether or not they understood that I was actually intelligent.

"I'm Alex Smith. Who are you? Are you nobody too?"

They didn't get the joke. "No humor!" I made a mental note to myself. I'd long since reached the point where I didn't really care anymore.

"So, what've we got on tap today?" I asked. "A little touchy-feely here, a little in-and-out maybe?"

Big Guy suddenly bent over me again and just stared. I really think it was trying to communicate, but it just wasn't getting through. I felt a sort of tickle in my mind. If I was interpreting its facial expression correctly, it was becoming frustrated by the effort.

It spoke something to one of the biped attendants, who brought it an instrument.

"Hoooo! Wait just a minute there!" I yelled, when I saw the thing.

It looked like some kind of laser gun to me. Someone on the other side abruptly grabbed my left arm and injected it. Another creature seized my head and put it into a vise of some kind, completely immobilizing it. I started getting numb again.

"Wh-what are y-you d-doing?" I mumbled, but they just proceeded in their very methodical way to prepare me for whatever indignities they intended to foster on my poor body.

One of them poked at me with a needle, and when I obviously couldn't feel the thing, looked over at Big Guy. There was a high-pitched sound as it turned on the instrument. Then they proceeded to remove the top of my skull (I spied the floppy salt-and-pepper hair when they lifted it off). I wasn't able to move a muscle.

Then Big Guy looked around at its colleagues, lifted up a half dozen tentacles, and very daintily probed my brain. Its eyes slowly closed as it bent to its work.

They say that your entire life flashes in front of you when you're dying. I don't know if that's true or not—it seems to me rather unlikely on the surface—but I do know that I felt my every experience, my feelings and thoughts and histories, my interactions, my encounters with the Martians, my sins and sorrows, my joys and triumphs, all being scooped out of my head, as if my brain were some hard drive full of data that could be reaped by an Internet pirate.

Everything that I was, everything that I'd done, everything that I knew, was hanging there before me in my mind—and was now also part of the Martian consciousness. I knew this, as surely as I knew that I was still alive.

Then Big Guy withdrew its feelers, and one of the other Martians—I called it Crook Mouth—put my head back together again and sealed the suture. I was taken away once more to the waiting or recovery room (I doubt if there was any equivalent in our culture), where I was injected with the anti-venom, and fed and watered and cleaned up again by the monkey-creatures. Once more I slept awhile.

When I awoke, Big Guy was sitting (?) there staring at me. Just staring. No one else was in the room. I could move again and see for myself. It loomed large over me, reached out a tentacle, and touched my forehead.

"Sah-Mit," it hissed.

It took me a second to realize that it was trying to say my name.

Then the main Martian touched the same tentacle to its forehead, and said: "Ah-Roohs-Tookh."

I understood!

"Aroostook," I said.

And that was all. It just got up and left the room, leaving me there with my mouth agape.

When I think back upon this strange, almost surrealistic series of events, I wonder what I could or should have done, if anything. Are our species so far apart, then, that no real communication is possible? I think that this encounter proved the fallacy of that argument, once and for all.

And yet...and yet, how does one explain what happened afterwards?

PART THREE
MARS RECUMBENT

You furnish the pictures and
I'll furnish the war.
—William Randolph Hearst

O God of battles! Steel my soldiers' hearts;
Possess them not with fear; take from them now
The sense of reckoning, if the opposèd numbers
Pluck their hearts from them.
—William Shakespeare

CHAPTER TWENTY-THREE
THE LADY OR THE TIGER?

No man chooses evil because it is evil;
He only mistakes it for happiness, the good he seeks.
—Mary Wollstonecraft

Alex Smith, 7 Bi-October, Mars Year VII
Beneath Nier Crater, Planet Mars

After that I slept for some time, and when I awoke I found that I was a stranger in a strange land. Somehow the buggers had moved me without me being aware of it. I waited for my attendants magically to appear, and when they didn't, decided to do a little exploring of my own. But the room was empty, and there was no sign of anyone. The Martians and their biped assistants had vanished.

I also found no evidence of my clothes or goods or backpack, and no food or drink or furniture or equipment or anything at all. I was lying on a table in a bare stone chamber with two possible exits.

Which was it to be, then: the lady or the tiger?

I glanced into both corridors, but they were as empty as the cave. I lay down again. Surely they must have left me some clue. I was important enough for that, wasn't I? They had singled me out, right? The problem was, I didn't know *why* they'd picked me over the others. With the Martians, you just never knew for sure, and that was one of the most frustrating elements of the entire business. I'd spent a dozen years trying to fathom the aliens, and in some ways I wasn't any closer now to answers than I'd been during the War of Two Worlds, "Aroostook" notwithstanding.

Then something caught my eye, a kind of flicker in the lighting. I looked up at it more closely. I shut my eyes for a moment to clear out the afterimages, and then I peered at the stone ceiling again. Sure enough, there was a slight rippling effect in play, a kind of pattern that I'd never noticed before. The question immediately arose, of course: was it just because I'd been so lacking in discernment that I'd not seen this before, or was it something entirely new? I had no idea, really, but it was a start.

They were like little waves of light moving from one end of the chamber to another, from one exit to another, if I was interpreting them properly. I got up again, and felt very carefully all around my head. So far as I could determine, all the parts were back in their appropriate places, leaving neither scab nor scar as testimony to the aliens' work. *Sacrés crustacés, l'homme du chauve-souris!*

Time to rock and roll.

I followed the lights for what I think was many hours, until I wearied of the pace and sat down against the wall of the tunnel, its cold, hard stone pressing against my back. It was terribly uncomfortable, but what was I to do? I must have slept again, because when I awoke, I found beside me a tube of the sugar-water, which I consumed most eagerly. After satisfying my thirst, I examined the container more closely, and realized that it was a gourd of some kind, probably generated naturally by one of the Martian plants. I took it with me when I moved on.

I don't know for certain how long I wandered in that wilderness of mazes and passageways, only that I consistently followed the pattern of the ceiling lighting. After a bit, I began to notice that I seemed to be moving uphill slightly. Twice more these little refreshments were left for me by unseen hands. I think I almost caught a glimpse of one of the bearers of sweet tidings right near the end, but it could have just been my imagination: I saw a flash of something like a large ferret. It made me think that we had barely even begun to plumb the mysteries of the Red Planet.

All of the tunnels that I'd been walking through had the appearance to me of side-passages. They were about six feet in diameter, with floors that were slightly uneven, not at all similar to the much larger corridors that we had traversed to enter the Martian underground. Occasionally, I would even stub a toe on a small stone, and I had seen no loose rocks whatever in the great byways of subterranean Mars. This told me that those structures must be maintained on a regular basis to keep them so clean.

Sometime during that long day I reached one of these main "drags," so to speak, and turned in the direction that the lights pointed me. I was very, very tired by now, but determined to go on until I reached my ultimate destination, whatever that was.

Then I saw the artificial pip of a lamp glowing off in the far distance, and I shouted as loud as I could, although my voice seemed to me the merest squeak by this time. I stumbled forward towards that beckoning beacon of hope, and was surrounded suddenly by my lost comrades.

"What happened to you?" they asked.

"Where have you been?"

"What have you seen?"

What could I say?

It was the lady or the tiger all over again.

CHAPTER TWENTY-FOUR
AND ON THE SEVENTH DAY

'Tis not the meat, but 'tis the appetite
Makes eating a delight.
—Sir John Suckling

ALEX SMITH, 7 BI-OCTOBER, MARS YEAR VII
BENEATH NIER CRATER, PLANET MARS

I was just about played out, but I managed to scarf down the goodies that somehow magically appeared in front of my face, including—*mirabile dictu!*—a chunk of real chocolate interlaced with deliciously divine divots of almonds. I suspect this came from the stash of General Fritz Burgess himself, for which kindness God bless his mercenary, military soul.

Someone found me some extra clothes that didn't really fit, and then I slept for a week, or at least it seemed that way to me. It actually must have been about eight or ten hours.

When I stirred again amongst the Land of Living Men, I packed in another meal, this time of the ubiquitous MREs, and was promptly marched off—"right, left, right, left"—to the Good General's tent to be debriefed.

What the military usually means by "debriefing" is the draining of just about everything of value from one's immortal soul. I told him—and I later told the scientists and members of the Advisory Council—all that I knew, which wasn't much, and all that I conjectured, which wasn't much more. They didn't seem to appreciate my sarcastic attitude at all. Indeed, they seemed downright suspicious of me, particularly after the previous incident.

But the thing was, I now realized for the first time what a fool's errand we were on. If we weren't real careful about things, we'd wind up destroying each other for lack of communication. I had no great confidence in the ability of either side to reach out to their opposites, despite my experience in the Martian lab, and I told them so. Again, they failed to approve either of my intelligence or my candor.

Finally, they had to let me go. There was no place to confine me down in the dungeons of the pit, and too few men really to guard me on a constant basis.

Mayer greeted me most enthusiastically afterwards, and we shared a meal together. Markus was at least cordial, but Reverend Lesley tried to avoid me at all costs. Once again, I had failed to match her view of the universe. I'd saved her worthless life almost at the cost of my own. In her own mind, that was *her* role. Of course, that would have required a mote of courage on her part. No matter.

They asked me not to attend the meeting of the rump Advisory Council. They'd been down in this godforsaken pit for seven days now, and had accomplished less than nothing. They were trapped like rats in a hole, but the Martians refused to reveal themselves to such idiots, and I didn't expect them to alter their ways just on our behalf. After all, this was *their* world and *their* home, and we were intruding upon it.

Finally, Burgess summoned me to appear.

"You stated," he said, "that the lights showed you the way. We haven't seen any lights down here."

"You can't see them," I said, "unless you open your eyes"— *and minds*, I added silently—"to them. They run at such a low intensity that you have to turn off everything artificial, and let your eyes adjust to the darkness. Then you'll see the illumination."

"Levine!" the General ordered, and the lamps went out.

Slowly the figures around me reappeared in the gloom of the Martian tunnel.

"I'll be fuckin' damned!" Mayer exclaimed from somewhere outside the tent.

"You also said in your testimony that there was a pattern to them," Burgess said.

"Well," I said, "it was obviously generated by the aliens to guide my way out of the maze. I don't know if they'll do the same for you."

"Well, look, damn you!"

So I looked, and sure enough, I could see the ripples of the guidance system that the Martians had provided for me.

"There!" I said, pointing at one part of the rounded ceiling.

Everyone stared, until finally Markus said, "I see it!"

Not everyone did, but there were enough to verify what I'd experienced.

"Where do you think it'll lead us?" Burgess asked.

"Haven't a clue. The Martians were never very big about telling me things. I sorta had to figure them out for myself. I'm hoping it's a way out of this mess, but I can't guarantee that, and you shouldn't hold it against me if we walk off into an abyss together."

"We'll try it anyway."

But we waited until the next day before proceeding.

That night the music came again, a gentle panoply of sound that washed over my consciousness and soothed me into a deep, refreshing sleep. I saw in my mind's eye a great pool of water, almost an underground lake, and in it floated Big Guy, the seven-foot-tall Martian.

"Go home," it said, waving a tentacle idly at me.

It sported an off-center beanie topped by a propeller canted to one side of its head. There was almost a grin plastered over the bottom of its large, silly face.

"We can't," I said.

"We've shown you the way."

"We're here for good."

"Not good," the Martian said, "not good for either of us."

"We have no way to go back."

"Ah," the alien hissed. "We have the same problem."

"What do you mean?"

"We can't go back either."

"I don't understand," I said.

"Yes."

Then its image was overlaid with the likeness of the leader of the biped creatures.

"We will kill you," it growled from deep within its narrow chest. "We will kill you all!"

And I wondered for the first time who was master and who was servant in the Martian universe.

CHAPTER TWENTY-FIVE
TO SEE AGAIN THE STARS

The best way out is always through.
—Robert Frost

ALEX SMITH, 8 BI-OCTOBER, MARS YEAR VII
BENEATH NIER CRATER, PLANET MARS

We started early the next day, beginning at the camp near the machine room, and then turned south down the cross corridor. We kept our ears open for any of the dome-vehicles speeding along the way, but heard nothing out of the ordinary. The tunnel continued straight onward for miles and miles on end, with never a deviation from its path.

Then the lights took us west in another way, and 'round and 'round and through and through we went, slowly plodding our journey amid the underground chambers and passages of the Martian civilization. We saw occasional mosaics and once a room full of discarded machinery, but nothing else that first half-day. We stopped for lunch and a rest break about noon.

During the previous hour or so we'd noticed that the air was getting cooler and the atmosphere a little lighter. Mayer found a spare breather for me to use, together with some gloves and a warm coat. I appreciated the gesture, and told him so, but he seemed to feel that he could never repay the debt that he owed me.

We started again about an hour later, and soon came upon

a chamber that was filled with the red weed and its cousins, through which wound a mosaic-lined pathway that wandered among the plants. Instead of pictures, the inset rocks and minerals displayed geometric patterns.

"Look over here!" Dr. Alan Scott exclaimed. "It's a kind of fungus, I think, maybe of the family Candelabras."

He held up a giant rose puffball with a dozen dangling yellow "puffettes" hanging off to either side, and just the movement of his hand distributed a cloud of pale pink spores all over him and everyone else. He promptly sneezed and the thing exploded, disintegrating completely.

"Oh, fuckers chuckers!" he blathered, and went back to scrounging around in the plants, searching desperately for another specimen.

On the other side of the room, Dr. Gene Markus was declaiming over a small creature that he'd found crawling and feeding on one of the plant leaves.

"This is an insect, I'm reasonably sure of it," he cooed, holding the foot-long, caterpillar-like purple thingie in his outstretched hand; it was covered with orange bristles and was assiduously trying to chew through his glove. "At least I think I'm sure. Well, it might be something else, you know."

He stroked its back, and it looked up at him with love and devotion and purred, it just purred.

"Put it back," the General said.

"But, sir, but…."

"Purr, purr, purr," went the beast.

"This is an important find, sir," Markus said. "Why, it might even be related to the Bicorporeal Bouncing-Betty Bug, *Eruca conchyliatus*, which is known to exist in thirty-seven distinct permutations, each of them having slightly variant markings etched upon their thoraxes—or is it thoraces, I can never remember which. Anyway, this new thing, which I will name *Inflata oratio burgessa* in your honor, is an extraordinary creature indeed."

The Martian crawler had now fastened itself on the exobiologist's arm, and was siphoning blood from his veins.

"Look," the officer said, "We just don't have any way of preserving or maintaining these things. Take as many photos as you can over the next thirty minutes, and then leave all the flora and fauna here where they belong."

Dr. Scott had found another goodie, a flower that was snapping back at him as he tried to pick it.

"Ouch!" he yelled, when it nipped him.

Mayer joined me where I was looking at an array of what appeared to be Martian fire-flowers set off to one side of the chamber.

"This is a garden, isn't it, sir?" he asked.

"I think so," I said, "or possibly an arboretum or zoo of some kind—it's never quite that clear-cut when you're dealing with the Martians. They could also be food, I guess, or something completely different. You just never know."

"It's still a beautiful place, sir."

"*I* think so. It has an inherent grace to it that we sometimes seem to miss on Earth. The Martians are slow, but steadiness gives them a certain gravitas."

"What's that, sir?" Mayer asked.

"There's a kind of inherent serene solemnity to them and their creations that I find lacking in my fellow man."

Then we were called to order again, and began marching out to "Georgia."

Towards dinner time we entered a passage that inclined steadily upwards, but hesitated to stop for the evening meal when we appeared to be so close to exiting our prison.

All this time we'd been trying the radio, but static interference had prevented us from making contact with the surface. Suddenly, however, one of the soldiers reported a com uplink.

"Nier Base calling Task Force Alpha," the speaker blared out, and we cheered at the sound.

"General Burgess here," our commander said. "Let me speak to Colonel Billy Nolan."

"It's a thrill to hear your voice again, sir," the noncom said.

"It's good to hear yours too, son."

When Nolan came on, the General briefed him on the situation.

"Do you have any idea where you are, sir?" the Colonel asked.

"Not really," Burgess said, "but it has to be fairly close for the signal to be this strong. Be ready for us when we emerge."

We broke then for supper, and after resting for an hour, moved on again, eagerly spiraling upwards towards the surface. Our excitement grew hour by hour. The air was getting downright cold now, so we all buttoned up. The atmosphere was still breathable, however, so we didn't have to resort to our suits yet.

There were seventy-two of us left of the ninety-eight men and women who had descended into Mars a week earlier. Several had gone missing and never returned, but most had died in various horrible ways. We had their tags and little else: we'd no choice but to leave the bodies behind.

On and on we tramped, winding steadily higher as the evening progressed. About midnight we found an obstruction blocking our way.

"What is it?" Burgess asked.

"Well, it's made out of metal," Major Levine said. "You know, I almost think that it might be a door of some sort."

If it was a door, it sure as hell hadn't been opened in a very long time. We put on our environmental suits before tinkering with it, and then tried to push and pry our way through the obstacle, but to no avail.

"General?" Levine said, shaking his head negatively.

"Blow the sucker!" our commander ordered.

"Yes, sir!"

Several of our special ops people set the charges along one edge of the structure, and we removed ourselves a safe distance back around a bend in the corridor. There was a loud whoosh and bang, and all the air went rushing out. Even before the hanging hunk of metal had cooled, we were pushing our way forward from the side of Nier Crater onto the interior plain.

"From there we came forth, to see again the stars."

CHAPTER TWENTY-SIX
THE SOFT IMPEACHMENT

As headstrong as an allegory on the banks of the Nile.
—Richard Brinsley Sheridan

ALEX SMITH, 11 BI-OCTOBER, MARS YEAR VII
ISIS STATION, PLANET MARS

We quite forgot ourselves in the joy of reunion, although I believe in retrospect that we made an error of judgment in doing so. The patina of the Martian underground quickly dropped away from our psyches with the renewed excitement of our homecoming, and we forgot some of the lessons that we'd learned down there in the School of Hard Knocks.

Nier Crater Base was just as we'd left it; the soldiers and shuttles were waiting to welcome us, if not exactly with open arms, at least with evident enthusiasm. I immediately contacted Becky and Mellie to reassure them about my safety, although I said very little about my experiences. General Burgess decided to abandon the crater for the present, save for a token observation post; the evacuation of our forces began first thing next morning and proceeded throughout the next day.

Of the Martians and their great machines there was no sign on the surface. The blowing sand and reddish soil mocked our determination to conquer this world, covering all of our sins quite effectively. I knew that we hadn't even begun the process of taming the aliens, if that was even possible (which I doubted);

we would have enough difficulties surviving the harsh climate of the Red Planet over the next two years.

By now I was thoroughly sick of the whole venture. Yes, the Martians had attacked us, and yes, they'd been defeated, and yes, they'd attacked us again, and yes, we'd attacked them once more, and, and…when or where would it end? When do you ever say, "Enough?"

Still, I was happy to be home again at Isis Station. They lifted us off from Nier Crater on the morning of the Ninth, and we were back at Isidis Planitia just two hours later. God, it was good to see my family once more! I just hugged and hugged them both—and they hugged me back—until I thought we would all drop.

"When I heard the expedition was trapped down below, I thought I would die," Becky said. "There was no word from any of you for over a week."

"Tell us what happened, Daddy," Mellie said.

But I couldn't, really. Some of the things were just too grim to bear repetition, even for me. I dream about them still sometimes. I hear the screams of the dying, I see the bipeds charging at me with their weapons, I wipe the blood of the pulverized soldier off my clothes, and I shudder deep within the night at all that I experienced. And most of all, I see the huge Martian I named Big Guy.

So I told them a story that was a trifle sanitized, but one they could hear without cringing at the damage to my soul—or to theirs. I related the wondrous things that I'd seen, and the tunes of the alien music, and the little opera in light and sound that had been played out just for me. I told them all those things, and some of them were even true.

General Burgess gave us several days to recover before calling the Advisory Council back into session. All the surviving members were present, either in person or displayed by video from Granick Valley Station and the two moon bases. He said:

"Ladies and gentlemen and officers, I've asked you to meet with me to discuss what should be done with the Martians.

We've already circulated some of the accounts of the team members, including Dr. Smith, whose experience with the aliens surpasses that of anyone else here. We've also passed out the various reports generated by the experts and the scientists who were present on the expedition, concerning the Martian civilization and the facts that are now known about it.

"I need to have your recommendations on the best course of action for the long-term survival, both of this colony and of our own world. We've tried meeting the enemy on his own terms, and we've basically failed to make contact. They don't appear to desire direct communication with us—or perhaps they're unable to do so. We…."

I interrupted.

"Sir, with all due respect, I do believe they want to commu-nicate, but they're telepathic by nature, and they've lost the sensibility or habit of verbal interaction. I saw them giving brief orders to their attendants, the mammal-like bipeds, so they do have some ability in that regard. It's just that I don't believe that they're used to interfacing on a higher plane with intelligent beings except through direct mental contact."

"But that still means that we can't communicate with them," Burgess said.

"No, sir, it does not! It means that we have to try a little harder at it. I *was* able to reach them, and them me, albeit in a very limited fashion. We started by exchanging names. That isn't much, I know, but it's potentially the beginning of some-thing bigger. I'd be willing to return to the caves and try again, since they seem amenable to dealing with me. Maybe that would result in an eventual breakthrough."

"No, Alex, no!" Becky said (she represented the Sensitives, although I don't think she was speaking on their behalf this time). "I won't have you going again."

Burgess cleared his throat.

"By your own account, Dr. Smith," he said, "you were attacked by one Martian species and dissected by another. You were shot at, paralyzed, injured, and nearly killed. I don't see very much promise there. If we sent you back, you'd likely never return, and I can't condone losing another valued member of our team."

I saw then the way that this would go.

"General Burgess," Dr. Mindon Min said (he represented the Scientists). "We don't know enough to make any decisions yet. The surface area of Mars is equivalent to all the land masses of Earth put together. We've not even begun to explore the rest of this world. We suspect there are additional Martian cities buried underground, maybe a network of them connected by these tunnels, but who really knows? They may even have bases in the Asteroid Belt.

"We need some hard facts, and while I respect your abilities and those of your fellow officers and men, I submit that we have to do much more exploration before we can hope to reach some consensus here."

"Well, Doctor, I'm not asking for your consensus," Burgess said, "only your suggestions. I still haven't been told anything that addresses our basic problems. Let me outline these:

"The first issue is the survivability of our bases. We have limited supplies of oxygen and water and food. Locating a good source of water could potentially take care of the other two requirements.

"Secondly, we've been subjected to several attacks by the aliens, and we're lucky to have escaped thus far with so little damage. We might not be so fortunate in the future if these depredations persist. My own belief is that they will, and that we have to be the aggressors if we're going to survive down here for very long. Our experiences in the Martian caverns simply reinforced this feeling.

"Thirdly, we have to stop the meteor bombardment of Earth before the invaders destroy our planet, which they will do, given enough time.

"So, while I'm always interested in your prognostications, touchy-feely solutions just won't work in my estimation. I'm not looking for good vibes or reverberations or a 'hands outstretched to our neighbors' social function. Give me some practical ideas, and I'll consider them."

Then he turned to my wife.

"What does *your* group say, Mrs. Smith?"

"*Ms.* Smith, if you please," Becky said. "Madame Stavroula believes that the Martians will defend themselves with everything in their power. They have no more wish to die than we do. They want us to leave their planet and go home. If we do this, they will stop sending the asteroids."

"Well, tell the good Madame for me," the commander said, "and her friends the Martians as well, that I wish we had that option. However, we're stuck here for at least two more years, and even then, there won't be enough transports available to ferry us back to Earth. Surely the aliens can understand this."

"They will allow you to withdraw unmolested to the Martian moons. You may continue to maintain observation posts there indefinitely."

"*Ms.* Smith, we don't have enough supplies to survive six months, much less two years, on the orbital stations. They would be terribly overcrowded, beyond any possibility of sustaining our entire population for the period in question. We have to find some basic resources down here on the surface, or we're all going to die. It's as simple as that."

Major Levine spoke up: "Sir, we know where the alien pits are located. We still have some of the Interference Runners left. We could activate the nukes that some of them carry, and plug up the Martian holes for a good long time to come. Maybe that would give us the time we need to locate a decent source of underground water."

"Folks," I said, "we're still missing a basic point here. If we attack the Martians, they'll likely respond in kind. This is their world, they know the territory, and they control all the options. Why not try establishing some basis for a long-term peace? It can't hurt, and if the effort succeeds, we'll have rescued both ourselves and our planet from oblivion. If it doesn't for some reason, all of the other possibilities are still open to us."

"The Martians are evil," Reverend Lesley blurted out (she represented the Chaplains). "They should be destroyed. God will not accept such heinous creatures into the Kingdom of Heaven. They can only be residents of the lower circles of Hell. We have a moral imperative to exterminate them. It's us vs. them. It's good vs. evil. It's right or wrong. It's white vs. black. There are no other options available to good Christian soldiers."

We continued to discuss the issues well into the evening, but reached no common conclusion. I was resigned to the outcome. General Burgess assured us, however, that he would consider our suggestions that night, and would give us his decision on the following day.

I went back to our cubicle in Barrack 7, where I talked with my wife and daughter into the wee hours of the morning.

"What's going to happen, Alex?" Becky asked.

"I don't know," I said, half disingenuously.

Mellie snuggled up next to me, and then looked into my eyes.

"Daddy, we mustn't go to war," she said. "We can't. They come to me in my dreams. They talk to me. The one you call Big Guy says they are much like us, living in many different nests. Some of them have—I don't know the words—they have leashes on some of the others. If we hurt them, though, they *will* hurt us back. We *have* hurt them already, and they have hurt us. There is a balancing now. If we make the balance go away, Big Guy does not know what will happen afterwards. Bad things, it thinks."

I stroked her soft hair.

"Tell me, Little One," I said, "Do you have any idea from your visions what or who Big Guy is?"

"It's not possible to describe this," she replied after a very long pause; she seemed to be in some kind of trance. "The, uh, the ideas, the notions are not there. Our minds are filled with chaos and dis-, dis-con-tin-u-i-ties, whatever that is. We cannot understand you well. We don't know why you act the way you do. We try to, uh, '*kohl*' at you, but you do not '*kohl*' back. We try to perform the '*ooh-lah*,' but you do not '*koh-vahs*.' We are saddened for you. You do not mesh with the whole. You do not find '*rohh*.' You are alone."

I pondered these thoughts for a very long time, but I could only make partial sense of them. I don't think the aliens really wanted war, but I knew that they wouldn't let us end their civilization. I wondered who else was out there, and how far and how long this conflict would continue if we took the next step. The soft impeachment of our lies and prevarications would soon find fertile soil.

Welladay, welladay, make a wish and go away.

I put Mellie to bed and told her the story of the purple Martian caterpillar and the orange puffball, and that sent her off to Slumberland in very quick order. Even Becky was hunched over in her chair, soundly snoring up a storm.

Then I began humming a tune of my own, a little ditty that wavered up and down the scale, that sang of ancient seas and elden lands, and the endless blowing of ruddy sands.

CHAPTER TWENTY-SEVEN
HURRAH! HURRAH!

Hurrah! Hurrah! We bring the jubilee!
Hurrah! Hurrah! The flag that makes you free!
—Henry Clay Work

ALEX SMITH, 12 BI-OCTOBER, MARS YEAR VII
ISIS STATION, PLANET MARS

Surprise! Surprise! It was war!

General Burgess called us together just before noon, and announced his decision.

"We'll commence bombing the Martian installations as quickly as possible, with an aim to destroying their basic infrastructure as much as we can. We realize that we're not going to reach some of their underground facilities, but we think that we can hamper their operations enough that we'll have time to build our bases up to self-sufficiency."

I raised my hand. "Sir, what if this doesn't work?"

"What do you mean, Smith?"

"Well, you're presuming a great many things that may or may not be true," I said (I was beginning to sound more and more like my wife, Becky). "Even our most powerful weapons won't penetrate very deeply beneath the surface. What if the aliens survive our assault, and then mount a counterattack?"

"You forget that we control the skies. Our orbiting Warstations will both warn and protect us against any large-scale operations by the Martians. Yes, we're still vulnerable to the occasional raid by one of their striders, although we've taken steps to mine all of the outlying areas surrounding our two stations. I think we're pretty safe at this point."

"You don't actually know that."

"No, Dr. Smith, but I can reasonably assume this from the information that all of you've given me." Burgess scratched his head in frustration. "Look, Doctor, we'll never know all the answers here. All I'm trying to do is find a way to protect ourselves from the Martians, and also to save our homeworld.

"In the meantime," the General said, deliberately changing the subject, "we're redoubling our efforts to find a sustainable source of water for our bases. We have some promising leads now, according to Dr. Andrews. I'll let him speak for himself on this subject."

A thin, gray-haired man in his fifties stepped forward.

"Well," he said, "we did ask the ladies to try some dousing"— he chuckled while Becky grimaced—"but they, uh, they claimed that it wasn't their forte, so we've just been doing some standard probing and digging of test wells in the lowest parts of the Isidis Planitia. We believe that this area was once a very large lake or an arm of the Great Northern Ocean of Mars, and that there may still be some residual pools of liquid buried beneath the surface layers. These may or may not be potable, but if we can locate even one large reservoir, we could, if necessary, treat the water to make it usable. Our soundings would suggest that a large cavern exists about fifty miles northeast of our campsite, and that's where we're currently concentrating our efforts."

"How soon before you penetrate the rock?" Mindon asked.

"I expect our test hole to produce results within a few days." And that was that.

After the usual pallid lunch in the Mess Hall, Mindon and I put on environmental suits and went outside for our first extended conversation together since my return. The station had changed considerably in the intervening two weeks. The Seabees had created a pair of permanent runways for the surveillance drones and shuttles to use. Although the shuttles could—and had—been used as VTOL craft during our operations at Nier Crater, actually landing them on the runway saved some small mote of fuel, particularly when they were transiting from one of our two Martian moon bases. We tried to conserve every resource whenever possible, because so much of what we had was essentially irreplaceable. The workers had also assembled some one- and two-man light flyers.

But the Seabees had made other refinements as well. We now had an actual electrified perimeter fence surrounding our base, complete with trenches, minefields, strider traps, reinforced guard posts, and other little surprises. HQ had also been fortified, two additional structures having been added to one side of the main module. I didn't know yet what they contained. A laser gun emplacement had been built on top of the covered central structure, where it could survey and protect the entire camp.

The hangers for the shuttles and half-tracks and other vehicles had been sunk into the ground and layered with rocks and dirt as additional protection against possible sting-ray or missile attacks (not to mention solar radiation). I could see more men and vehicles continuing to add to our infrastructure even as we watched.

"We're here to stay, aren't we?" I said.

"I think so, Alex, although the Marties might have something yet to say about that."

"Remember that night in Novato years ago when we were watching the initial launching of the Martian spaceships through your telescope? What was that girl's name? You know, Blondie or Boopsie?"

"You mean Brio?" He laughed out loud. "I think there was more than one of them there that night. But Brio was certainly part of the group. She was the one who asked me about my real name. Ha!"

"What happened to your latest girlfriend?" I asked.

"You mean Puff? Just got a message from her the other day. She keeps threatening to come out on the next expedition two years hence. I really like Puff. Might even be willing to settle down with her at some point. If they don't let her fly, maybe I'll just go back home myself."

"You think?" The suit and breather had deepened my voice. "Then I'd never see you again. I'd have no one to talk to."

"Hey, would that be such a terrible thing?" Mindon was waxing philosophical. "We've known each other for, what, twenty or more years now? I mean, I don't have any new jokes to tell you, man. Don't even feel much like jokes anymore."

"Me either," I said. "This damned war is just going to get worse before it gets any better. I really think we're heading down the wrong road here. Don't know *how* the Martians will respond."

"*They* already know."

"What do you mean?"

"Jeez, Alex, haven't you ever thought about the reality of telepathy, of how it would actually work?"

"It's hard to envision such things when you have no control over them. I just have these dreams, Min, just these weird visions in my sleep. Half the time, I don't even know what they mean, if they mean anything at all."

"It's gotta be a two-way street. If you're getting something from them, what are they getting from you?"

I hadn't thought of it that way.

"Oh, shit!" I said.

"Oh, shitty shit, shit, indeed! So, I figure they already know—have known at every stage, really, ever since we've been on this godforsaken world—they know exactly what we intend and where and how and so on. You're not *ever* going to surprise them. They're only going to surprise us. I mean, they control the filtering process. They let you see what they want you to see. Isn't that the truth? Hey, man, who the fucking hell really knows!"

"Then it's all subjective, every bit of it. We don't know what's real and what isn't in this Alice in Wonderland world."

"Look how they manipulated you guys down in that hole of

theirs," Mindon said. "Think about what you've told me and the Council. Did you have *any* real control over *any* of those events? I don't think so. I think they were playing you all along. The only question is: do they, or did they, mean well or not?"

This conversation was making me increasingly uncomfortable. I could see permutations of my own experiences that I hadn't even considered before. I looked out at the distant, craggy mountain peaks for a very long time indeed before finally replying.

"I think that the one whom I called Big Guy—Aroostook—I think that that was genuine," I said. "I think that I'd have known if there'd been any false notes there. The connection was intimate enough that some things just couldn't have been hidden."

"You think!"

"Yes, I *think*, Min." I sighed. "But the rest of it, well, Christ, I don't know. Maybe Madame Stavroula really does have a better connection to the 'ætherweb.' I haven't had much contact with her since we arrived. She's the antithesis of everything I believe in."

"No," Mindon said, "Reverend Lesley is."

"Yeah, you're right again. I don't care much for the 'Holy Ghost.' I saved her life down there, so we're even now, at least as far as I'm concerned. I don't feel guilty any more about her nearly dying while in my care during the War of Two Worlds."

"Some of the others in that bunch are much more down to earth. Father Phil, for example, over in Granick Valley: I met him the other day when he was visiting here as part of an official delegation from that station."

"Father Phil, huh? I've heard that name somewhere before. Wasn't he a singer, a baritone or a soprano or something?"

"That would have made him a castrato!" Mindon said, laughing. "I don't think he falls into *that* category."

I changed the subject once more: "I wonder how long before they start bombing the Martian pits again?"

"Pretty soon, I expect. Maybe later tonight or early tomorrow."

"How many of those things have they still got left?"

"Dozens, from what I hear. They used a few of them around the time of our landing, but at least half of the original complement still remains in orbit."

"Then God help the Martians!" I said.

"God help us all!"

"Each and every one!"

CHAPTER TWENTY-EIGHT
BOMBS AWAY!

And the rockets' red glare, the bombs bursting in air,
Gave proof through the night that our flag was still there.
—Francis Scott Key

ALEX SMITH, 15 BI-OCTOBER, MARS YEAR VII
ISIS STATION, PLANET MARS

But it was actually October the Thirteenth before the orbital bombardment of Mars started anew.

Once again the known Martian bases and weapons emplacements were the primary targets. Most of these were located within the walls of very large craters. Everyone was able to watch the proceedings live on the telenet directly in their own rooms, although the images were also broadcast in the dining halls and community centers. The cameras mounted on the orbiting Warstations captured the engagement remarkably well.

Both nuclear and conventional explosives were employed. Our forces began by softening up the targets with the nukes, blasting large holes in the entrance pits of the alien camps. The Interference Runner satellites were then crashed down onto the interior surfaces of the craters, generating huge clouds of dust and massive fireballs. No secondary explosions were noted, although some of the structures did collapse slightly inward, indicating that the caverns beneath them had been destroyed.

The operation continued all that day and into the night. We

used every available remaining major weapons package, except those that were reserved for orbital defense against any future attacks by the Martian spaceships. As General Burgess said, "This is not the time to hold anything back."

When the dust finally cleared on the Fourteenth, all that remained of the seven identified Martian bases was a series of massive holes in the ground. Even the surrounding crater walls had largely been devastated.

Burgess announced "mission accomplished" over the station com, stated that the operation had been a "great success," and thanked "all of the brave members of the United States Space Force for their joint efforts in beating the Martians." A day of thanksgiving was proclaimed on both stations, both moon bases, and back on Earth as well. Most everyone was walking around with a self-satisfied smirk plastered on his or her face.

And that wasn't the only good news that we received. Dr. Andrews's borehole finally hit pay dirt on October the Fifteenth, finding a large pool of brackish water buried a thousand feet beneath Isidis Planitia. The liquid gold appeared to be easily retrievable and could be treated for drinking purposes, and also to irrigate the hydroponics lab. The Seabees immediately set about laying a pipeline from the drilling site to our facility, and fortifying the new structures with extensive defensive perimeters. We would have fresh water again within a couple of weeks!

The Martians remained quiet during the immediate aftermath of our bombardment. My dreams ceased to disturb my sleep, and even Mellie was able to get a good night's rest. Maybe the aliens had gone away, or at least had decided that tangling with the crazy foreigners wasn't an especially productive idea.

Some wag began producing screensavers displaying Martian craters with bright red targets overlaid on them. Variations included images of the aliens themselves, covered by a red circle with a line through it. Other "clever" messages proclaimed: "The only good Martian is a dead Martian!" or "Kill a Martian first thing in the morning—take the rest of the day off!" or "Stomp a Martian if you love Jesus!" or "Marsburgers—overcooked and underfried!"

The Mars Gazette, our homegrown virtual newspaper, trumpeted: "VICTORY IS OURS!" The ensuing article featured detailed interviews with General Burgess and the other military macho-men, as well as a statement from President Bush and her Veep, the ex-Governor of California.

The latter appeared in a choreographed press conference on the steps of the Capitol Building back in D.C., holding an Uzi in one hand and brandishing a cigar in the other.

"We've met the enemy," he said, "and he is ours! We've kicked their fat Martian butts from San Francisco and Los Angeles all the way back to the oozing pits of Utopia Planitia. Once again, truth, justice, and the American way have triumphed over good and evil, just as they will in Iraq, Iran, Saudi Arabia, Lebanon, Syria, Egypt, Afghanistan, and Albania. These alien girly-men have been driven back to their Neanderthalish caves. The Red, White, and Blue flag now flies proudly o'er the Martian plains. Let's hear it for our brave boys and girls in blue! Today, Mars—tomorrow, the universe!"

I wanted to send him a note pointing out that the uniforms of "our brave boys and girls" on Mars were actually a dull red, designed that way to blend in with the planetary terrain here; however, I don't think he actually ever read anything, so perhaps this would have been a futile exercise, although it would have made me feel a whole lot better.

And so it went, both on Mars and on Earth.

Men have a way of congratulating themselves over the smallest details of their existences, of stating the obvious in such a blatantly offensive manner as to eliminate any regard that individuals might have either for them or for their real accomplishments.

We should have waited a bit.

We should have known better!

CHAPTER TWENTY-NINE
DUST UNTO DUST

For dust thou art,
And unto dust shalt thou return.
—Bible, *Genesis 3:19*

ALEX SMITH, 30 BI-OCTOBER, MARS YEAR VII
ISIS STATION, PLANET MARS

It began as a small atmospheric disturbance near the Martian North Pole, so reported on October the Fifteenth by the *San Francisco*, one of our orbiting Warstations. Somewhere adjacent to the ruins of Lomonosov Crater, a minor vortex began to form. The cloud had the appearance initially of a little puff of white smoke against the reddish backdrop of the Vastitas Borealis, the great, globe-encircling plain that abuts on the polar region to the north and on the Utopia Planitia in the south; indeed, some researchers consider the latter merely an extension of the ancient dry ocean bed.

No one knew exactly why such tempests formed in the thin air of Mars. Back in the twentieth century, our early orbiters had recorded an immense disturbance that had obscured the entire surface of the Red Planet for several years; rather curiously, it'd formed right after one of our observation satellites attained Mars orbit. Most of the storms, however, were of much shorter duration, and had a significantly lesser impact.

By the Twentieth the hurricane (for that's what it looked like by then) had grown to a swirling mass of vapor hundreds of miles in diameter.

By the Twenty-Fifth the size of the storm had reached a thousand miles and encompassed an increasingly large area of the open, unimpeded surface of northern Mars.

And by the penultimate day of the month, Isis Station and its sister base at Granick Valley were both beginning to feel the effects of the growing sandstorm.

It started first as a light breeze from the northeast, but by 0900 the wind had reached twenty MPH, and was beginning to pick up some of the red, loose soil of the old sea basin. General Burgess immediately called an emergency session of the Advisory Council.

Dr. Troy Walters, our resident meteorologist, gave us an overview of the situation.

"If you'll look at this display," he said, pointing to the map posted behind him (the session was also being televised and transmitted throughout our colonies, as well as off-planet), "you'll see this set of isobars, here, that indicate a rapid falling-off of the atmospheric pressure at the very center of the storm."

"What's causing this, Professor?" Burgess asked.

"Well, we don't truly understand how the great hurricanes on Mars actually form. The last really large disturbance occurred before we had any probes stationed on the planet's surface. There have been a few minor events since then, but we suspect that these humungous babies are something a little bit different."

"Could the Martians have initiated the process?"

"In theory, if you could suck the air down through a large pipe interface and impart simultaneously a severe rotational torque to the upper reaches of the cyclonic stack, you might be able to effect...."

"In laymen's terms, please, Professor."

"Well, maybe."

"Great. Where's this thing going, Walters?"

"Uh, it rather looks as if, um, well, maybe everywhere, sir," the scientist said.

"How many knots are we talking about?"

"I don't know, sir, and that's the honest truth. But I sure as hell would start battening down the hatches, and right away. This thing could grow to enormous proportions very, very quickly, and we'd all better be ready for it when it comes."

"Thank you, Professor. Comments, anyone?"

Burgess gazed around the table; we were meeting in the new conference room of the Administrative Complex at HQ.

"Nothing, Dr. Smith?" he asked, looking pointedly at me.

"You already know what I think, sir."

"Oh, I could probably guess," he said sarcastically. "Something about 'I told you so'."

"Indeed," I said. "Not that any of that matters now. What matters is our survival. We have to take steps immediately to secure both stations. We don't know how long this will last—it could literally be years—and during that time we're not going to be able to fly our shuttles or run our half-tracks or do much of anything, really, other than sit pat. So I would suggest, most generally and respectfully, sir, that we concentrate on identifying whatever additional supplies we might need right away, and have them transported down from either Phobos or Deimos."

"My God, the man actually has a practical streak to him! Will wonders never cease?" Burgess said. "In any case, I agree. Let's get cracking, everyone. We have a lot of work to do in a very short time."

The rest of the day was spent in a frenzy of mad activity. All the loose equipment and vehicles were stowed in secure bunkers. Half of the shuttles were moved up to the Martian lunar bases, where they'd remain for the duration of the crisis. We had ten loads of supplies dropped at both surface stations, including additional food, medicine, specialized replacement parts, a second reactor, communications gear, and weapons, as much of everything as we could possibly store.

The Seabees worked their collective asses off, trying to make certain that all the structural supports at both camps were solid enough to hold in a gale. More tunnels were laid in a frenzy of digging and construction out to the storage buildings, so we'd have access to them without having to chance any surface routes. But there was just so much that we could do before the winds reached dangerous proportions, and that occurred about midnight.

By then the weather gauges read almost 160 kilometers per hour, or roughly 100 MPH, and the sand was kicking up something fierce. Of course the atmospheric pressure was very light by Earth standards, but so was the fineness of the sand—it seemed to penetrate everything. One of the last shuttles to lift off reported erosion to its windshield, although it made the journey safely to Phobos. We could hear the howling of the wind even inside our buried cubicle in Barrack 7.

Fortunately, the new water system had been put in place just before the storm had mushroomed to its present dimensions. The well itself and the large pumping system were both totally automated, and the new pipeline from the excavation site provided us with an almost unlimited supply of salty water. A treatment facility had been included with our original supply modules, so we were up and running with our distillation plant before the first serious gusts really started to hit. All of our facilities were buried safely out of harm's way, and should survive even an extended period of isolation.

We were snug as a bug in a rug, and ready to last a long siege, if necessary. We figured the Martians would be as immobile as we were, so we really didn't worry too much about further attacks. Everything was on hold until the storm passed. Even if the aliens *had* created the tempest—and no one knew, really— they had impeded themselves as much as they had hamstringed us.

The only thing that really bothered me was the complete severing of communications between the Martians and the Sensitives. All of the dreams and visions had abruptly ceased after our bombardment of the alien bases.

Why? Were the aliens irretrievably pissed off? Or had we really damaged their infrastructure in some significant way?

We just didn't know.

These doubts nagged me all through that long day, just as they had plagued my mind during the previous weeks. I shared my concerns with Mindon and Becky and several others with whom I was conversant, but no one had any idea of what was happening. Even Madame Stavroula had ceased her prognostications.

"They will speak to us when they speak to us," she told me in passing. "All of you men see them merely as reflections of yourselves. You think that *they* think just as you do. You're wrong, you know. They have deep, intertwining thoughts that twist and turn down strange, unfathomable pathways."

"Do you think they made this perfect storm?" I asked.

"Oh, yes. They started this, and they'll finish it too. Ashes to ashes, dust unto dust. There's a kind of symmetry to it all, isn't there?"

And then something occurred to me that I hadn't thought of before.

I ran off to tell General Burgess, not that he could do much about it.

CHAPTER THIRTY
EL DÍA DE LOS MUERTOS

The worst is death,
And death will have his day.
—William Shakespeare

ALEX SMITH, 31 BI-OCTOBER, MARS YEAR VII
ISIS STATION, PLANET MARS

We got the call at 0600 the next day: Granick Valley Station was under attack. Each member of the Advisory Council was rousted out of bed by an M.P. and hurried through the long corridors to the conference room in the Administration Building.

The messages came first to our Control and Command Center, and then were piped to our meeting room. I could already hear the voices blaring when I walked into the chamber at 0635 on that last day of October.

"...Another hit. That last one was close to Station HQ. Colonel Nolan has ordered the civilian population into the equipment bunkers. If necessary, we'll sacrifice some of the birds to make"—[static]—"think they're using their cannons or striders to lob large boulders into the"—[static]—"says we've had a breach of Block 106. All pressure there has been lost."—[a huge thumping sound]—"Damn, that was close! The whole place shook. Musta weighed a quarter ton at least.

"Uh, just a moment, please, sir. The Colonel has just arrived and wants to talk right away with General Burgess."

"Yes, Bill," our commanding officer said.

"Sir, we've got a major problem here," came the static-filled response. "Our lasers just won't work under these conditions. The blowing sand scatters the light. Our missile tracking systems are having similar difficulties locking onto targets. Visibility is down below a quarter mile. We've fired at two Martian machines and taken out at least one, but the other retreated out of range. When we tried to pursue it with several of the half-tracks, they, well, they just vanished. We lost contact with them after a few minutes. They must have been destroyed.

"We have"—[static]—"fight back with. Can you provide us with any support at all?"

"I'm sorry, Bill, but the shuttles can't fly in this weather. We can't reach you via the surface, and the Warstations can't see you at all. Their lasers are as ineffective as yours."

"What about"—[static]—"missiles?"

"They can't achieve target locks with the interference," Burgess said. "There's nothing I can do. You're on your own."

"Then we'll do the best we can, sir. Nolan out."

Burgess shook his head and just sat there, his mouth hanging open. He looked at each of us in turn, but we had nothing to add that would help. Then he came to me.

"Is there anything you or the ladies can do to reach the Martians?" he asked.

"Sir, it's like the line has been severed," I said. "It's a dead zone."

"Ms. Smith?"

"I've asked my group about this," she said, "and they're at a loss as to what to do. Madame Stavroula says that a shade has been drawn between us. The aliens don't want to talk to us right now. The time for talking is past."

We received sporadic reports all that morning from Granick Valley, but the situation there just continued to deteriorate. They'd lost most of their residential buildings and several of their storage facilities. HQ was abandoned after a glancing blow from a large rock cracked the roof of the facility. Several hundred people had been injured, and at least twenty were dead, with many others unaccounted for. They were gradually and systematically being pounded into the dust.

Colonel Nolan was lost about midday on a foray to attack the attackers. He led six half-tracks out the main gate and disappeared into the swirling clouds of Martian soil, never to be seen again. I think they probably cracked the suckers like oversized eggs.

The beauty of the alien weapon was that it required nothing more than stealth and energy to activate. If you could launch heavy objects with impunity, even if your targeting system was no better than the enemy's, you could gradually reduce him to smithereens. And that's exactly what the Martians were doing to us.

Sometime late that night we lost all communication with Granick Valley. The *San Francisco*, orbiting high above the storm, received several static-filled transmissions between midnight and one the next morning, the gist of which seemed to be that the station's electrical grid was failing, most of its storage compartments had been breached, including their water containers, HQ had been destroyed, and the highest ranking officer now left alive was a Marine Lieutenant named Darcy Garrett. He sounded about twenty years old during his last relayed com message.

"S-sir, I don't know"—[static]—"failing"—[static]—"think they're c-coming through the"—[static].

And that was that.

Granick Valley had fallen to the Martians, and the people there were obviously dead, or soon would be. Five hundred men, women, and children, all gone in a day, the Day of the Dead, All Souls' Day.

I said a prayer for the repose of their departed souls, and wondered, oh I wondered, while gazing upon the drawn faces of my dear wife, I wondered if we were next.

CHAPTER THIRTY-ONE
SREDNI VASHTAR

Sredni Vashtar went forth,
His thoughts were red thoughts and his teeth were white.
His enemies called for peace, but he brought them death.
Sredni Vashtar the Beautiful.
—Saki

ALEX SMITH, 1 BI-NOVEMBER, MARS YEAR VII
ISIS STATION, PLANET MARS

But, as it happened, it was the *San Francisco* that was next.

The great Warstations had been maneuvered into geosynchronous orbits around Mars for two reasons: firstly, to provide a cover for our landing operations and some support for our subsequent offensive actions against the aliens; and secondly, to interdict the world to prevent any Martian ships from either entering or leaving the Red Planet's atmosphere.

In both functions they had served admirably.

We also had permanent bases on the two Martian moons, Phobos and Deimos, which orbited at different heights and circled the globe at different speeds from each other. These base structures were also partially protected by a fleet of shuttles and pods, and by the interposition of the moons themselves.

But everything relied on the maintenance of the basic defensive framework that we'd established. Pull out one leg of the structure and the rest would come tumbling down.

On Thursday we received a flash message from the *San Francisco*, which was the satellite permanently stationed over our section of Mars. Something had just been fired at it from the surface, probably a small projectile (a rock, truth be told), and they couldn't pinpoint the source. It was just too small—and the flight path wasn't apparent until it had cleared the dust cloud below.

A second missile then hit the structure, creating a small hole that was easily patched. And so it continued throughout the day.

We began getting reports from the other Warstations of similar incidents.

The *Bogotá* was impacted in one of its living quarters, with the death of twelve Marines. The *Fontana* lost some communications gear. The *Spokane* had a control jet destroyed. The *Wichita* received a glancing blow from a very large rock; they weren't really sure of their damage level yet; they'd have to send out a spacewalking party to make sure.

But the telling blow came when we received a *communiqué* around six that night saying that the *San Francisco* had exploded, with all hands lost. No one knew exactly what had happened, although Phobos Base speculated that one of the projectiles had hit a fuel storage bunker on the station, generating a spark that had set off the entire supply.

General Burgess called me to his private quarters after dinner. When I entered, he motioned me to sit down. The man had aged years in just a few days. One of his hands now had a persistent nervous tic in the small finger. He burped constantly as we talked, and popped several antacids.

"I, uh, I've called you here," he said very slowly, the fatigue showing in his gravelly voice, "I've called you here, Smith, because we have to do something to retrieve this situation. The Martians have outsmarted us again, as they always seem to do. We've obviously met our match. Operation Crimson Storm is on the edge of becoming a disastrous, horrendous failure.

"We basically mortgaged the future of our planet to generate this expedition in the first place. You know that. There's some real question about whether we can do it again in two years, even though the work's already been started.

"I don't expect the satellite stations to survive more than a week, any of them. They're all being targeted by these pellet-guns. I'm about to order them all to retreat to a safe distance from the surface.

"Our own station won't survive more than a few days if the aliens mount the same kind of attack that they mustered against Granick Valley.

"Surely there must be some way of communicating with the critters, of ending this madness before we're all dead. I've come to you because I don't know what else to do. You've had more direct contact with the Martians than other individual in the history of mankind. If anyone can find a solution, you can. You can have anything you want, any of our men or resources, anything that might help resolve this impasse. You have only to ask."

It was hard for me to see the man so beaten down, even if he deserved it. The arrogance of the military high command and of our political leaders had brought us all, had brought our very planet, to the precipice of destruction. But what could I do? I'd tried to reach out to the Martians, and had seemingly made some contact there, but it never had gone anywhere.

"What can I do?" I said out loud.

"I don't know, Smith, I really don't," came his weary reply, "but if you can't find something, and soon, that beautiful wife and daughter of yours will die along with the rest of us. Don't do it for me, son. Do it for them!"

He was right, of course. I had all the motivation in the world right before me. But the other thing was, I didn't really want to leave. I didn't want to go back to a planet so filled with corruption and guile and complication. Mars was purer somehow. Mars burned brightly with the red flame of simplicity.

It was only a utopia if we could make it one. We had the men and women and, yes, the Martians, to fashion a new world of cooperation and communication and the commingling of cultures, talents, and peoples. All of it was waiting for us there in that room of hallowed hopes, if only we could find the key to unlock the door.

"I'll do what I can," I said. "I'll kill the legacy of Sredni Vashtar."

"Who the hell's Sredni Vashtar?" the officer asked.

"Just an old dreary beast that I know," I said.

CHAPTER THIRTY-TWO
THE FOGGY, FOGGY DEW

And the only, only thing I did that was wrong
Was to keep her from the foggy, foggy dew.
—*The Foggy, Foggy Dew*

ALEX SMITH, 4 BI-NOVEMBER, MARS YEAR VII
ISIS STATION, PLANET MARS

The wind hurled its rage at us, bombarding Isis Station with gusts that now reached 130 MPH according to the base anemometer; but as yet there were no signs of the Martians. The next day General Burgess ordered the surviving Warstations hanging high above the Red Planet to retreat to safer orbits. Once they moved beyond Phobos, the pellet attacks on them abruptly ceased. "That far, and no more," the aliens seemed to be telling us.

We daily expected an assault on Isis Station, but none came.

I began to wonder if the reason why we'd thus far been immune to any serious incursion by the enemy was that our facility was the one place where the Sensitives had congregated. Granick Valley had been purely a military base, as had the distant Warstations. All of the civilian population that we'd shipped to Mars lived at Isis Station.

But were the aliens even aware of such distinctions? Did they care? Were they actually individuals in the same sense that we were? I needed more information before I could decide upon the best course of action. Whatever I did might be the last roll of the dice, so to speak, for all humanity.

A few days later, I was pondering what to do next when Mellie came plowing through the entrance-cloth of our cubicle, laughing and yelling and being chased by another preteen from one of the adjoining barracks.

"Slow down!" I ordered.

"Sorry, Daddy," she said, and then raced outside once more.

Becky appeared a moment later.

"It's good to see her acting normally again," my wife said. "I was worried about her for such a long time. The alien dreams just ate her up inside."

I'd paid too little attention to such details over the past weeks and months, and I knew it.

"How many kids does she have to play with?" I asked.

"Maybe a dozen her age. They're scattered all over the facility. She really misses her friends back on Earth. She gets e-mails and tweets and video-mails from them, of course, but it's not the same. She's at an age where a lot of things are happening in her life. She didn't really want to stay in Novato by herself, but I don't think she likes it here very much either."

"What about you, Becky?" I said. "Do *you* like it here?"

"I'd probably enjoy it more if you were actually *here* part of the time, Alex. I miss our conversations. I miss having meals together. I miss the little give-and-take that we always enjoyed. I just miss being with you."

There was another squeal in the corridor, and two sets of footsteps went racing by outside. I motioned to my wife, who came and sat on the edge of the chair. I put my arm around her, and held her close for a minute.

"I may have to go away again," I finally said.

She stiffened in my grasp.

"But I need your help to decide—and the aid of all of the Sensitives. Can you assemble them in the Mess Hall this afternoon with a few others of our friends?"

"If that's what you wish," she said.

"It's not what I want, so much as what I have to do."

I told her then about my last conversation with General Burgess.

"But what does he think you can do?" she asked. "*What*, Alex? You're not a miracle worker. You're just a man, a good man, yes, but…."

"I have to try," I said. "There's a reason why I'm here, I'm sure of it. I'm more certain of that now than ever before. I have a destiny to fulfill."

But before I could say more, the klaxons erupted in all their glee and the loudspeakers blared, "Orange Alert! The Station is under attack! All personnel report to their emergency posts!"

"We have to go," I said.

We kissed briefly, and then quickly hurried off to the conference room in the Administration Building at Station Headquarters.

The foggy, foggy dew was about to envelop us all.

CHAPTER THIRTY-THREE
DOWN AMONG THE DEAD MEN

It is well that war is so terrible,
or we should grow too fond of it.
—Robert E. Lee

Alex Smith, 4 Bi-November, Mars Year vii
Isis Station, Planet Mars

The Martians were pounding at our gate! And they weren't being particularly nice about knocking first.

When we reached the conference room in HQ, no one else was there yet. Captain Wells popped his head in briefly.

"The General's out on the perimeter. They're attacking our guard posts."

"Striders?" I asked.

"I, uh, I think so, sir. I've got to go."

The other members of the Advisory Council started showing up a few minutes later.

I put the station com on speaker, but all we got was a confused jumble of overlapping voices and yells and, sad to say, even screams.

"Got one!" somebody shouted.

"Number Six, report!" Burgess's voice ordered.

"Tank's coming up now, sir."

"I want information! Information!"

"Fire!"

"You won't get it!"

"Number Ten's been hit!"

"Pull back!"

"Lieutenant Michaels's down."

"They've breached the fence between Seventeen and Eighteen."

"Watch out! Watch out!"

"The fighting-machine's crippled. It fell across the perimeter wire."

"Whadya say?"

"Repeat!"

And finally, "They're retreating! Hold your fire!"

An hour later General Burgess finally appeared at HQ, disheveled and out of breath.

"Well," he said, "we beat them back this time, but if they come again, I don't think we can hold them very long."

The main problem we faced was the visibility. The Martians were able to approach very close to our line without being either seen or heard. Even though they couldn't employ their sting-rays in this kind of sandstorm, the striders themselves were formidable opponents. Despite our many traps and minefields, and the fierce resistance of our soldiers, several of the great tripods had almost breached our fence.

"There must have been a dozen or more of them out there," the General said. "I've never seen so many fighting-machines gathered together in one place before. They have to be bringing them in from everywhere. We're trying to do emergency repairs on the damaged guard posts, but the Seabees are having great difficulty working in these gale force winds."

"How tall were the machines?" I asked.

"Tall? What difference does that make? Oh, very well: maybe twenty feet in height."

"That's what I thought," I said. "They've modified them to adjust to the strong winds. The taller versions would have easily been toppled over by the heavier gusts."

"So they're adaptable," Burgess said. "I don't see how that

helps us."

"Well, they're still bound to be bit top-heavy in this type of weather. You might try putting some cats out there. All they'd have to do is catch one of those three legs and pull them off balance. Then they're vulnerable again."

Burgess paused for a moment.

"You know, that just might work."

He rushed off suddenly to C&C, and began shouting out a series of orders.

I threw up my hands.

"Can't do much more here, folks," I said. "I've got a meeting of my own to attend. Talk to you all later."

The ladies were waiting for us in the mess hall, together with Min, Zee, and Mellie. I raised one eyebrow, but I trusted Becky's judgment in these matters.

I gave them the gist of my earlier conversation with our commander.

"The problem is," I said, "that we have to find some way of reaching these creatures. We've all managed to make tentative attempts at communication with the aliens, but if we don't actually exchange some information in real time real soon, our tenure here is apt to be very short.

"I know that most of you have more or less experienced dreams or visions emanating from the Martians. I don't know about you, Min, and Zee has always been somewhere else anyway. But I've certainly had my share of the 'messages.'

"Then all of these interfaces stopped, just like that, right at the time we began conducting our final bombardment of the alien encampments. Does anyone know why?"

Zee appeared to be dozing in a chair off to one side. He opened an eye and looked at me.

"W-we d-dis-r-rupted their u-unity," he said.

"OK," I said. "So, how do we get it back again?"

"Y-you m-must g-go to-to-to-to them."

"But how do I find them?" I asked, gazing at each of them in turn. "Where are they? Even if I could reach Nier Crater, the entrance to the pit there has been destroyed by our weapons."

"L-let th-them f-f-f-find y-you."

"I think Zee's right," Mindon said. "They've been living on this planet for probably a billion years. They obviously have ways of getting around through the sandstorms and traveling to distant parts of this world. The Martians will find you if they want to find you—and if they don't, Alex, then we're probably all going to die, because all they have to do is just close us off here and let us rot.

"They don't even have to conquer us as such. As long as that storm is howling out there, they control all the variables, and we can't stop it. If they started the hurricane, they might be able to pull it back again, if they choose to do so. We have to provide them with some good reason to make that choice. In order to do *that*, we have to be able to talk to them.

"You're the only person here who's been able to interact with the aliens on some personal level. Maybe they'll let you do it again—you know, for old time's sake!"

Madame Stavroula then asked for the floor.

"Min's right—and wrong," she said. "Dr. Smith, when we met during the War in San Francisco, you didn't even recognize me without my makeup and costume, even though you'd seen me once before. I remembered *you*, even then; but like so many men, you displayed a selective blindness in your perceptive arrogance of self.

"We should both go. I've had the most, um, intimate visions from the Martians. Maybe it's my nature. I think they could access my mind better. Yours is just too stodgy. It's closed to new ideas. By yourself, you're not going to get anywhere with them."

"And you are?" I asked. "They didn't come for you. They didn't even draw you here, Nomsah. They sure as hell did me, though. I had absolutely no choice in the matter, and you know it. You haven't had one valid conversation with any of them, have you? You've received a lot of information, granted—and that's great. It's helped us all to figure things out. But they don't want you."

Then my daughter Mellie spoke up.

"No, Daddy," she said in her quiet little voice, "they want me. They want *me*, Daddy! You gave me their blood. You made me one of them. I bleed now, and now they want me!"

Well, folks, you could've heard the proverbial pin drop after that. The thing was, all of these people were Sensitives of one form or another, even me. Every one of them had a connection to that "Otherworld" out there. You can call it all psychobabble, you can label it sheer nonsense, you can say any damned thing that you want about it, but you can't explain who they were and what they did and how they received data in any other way. They were psychics, one for all, and all for one.

And the reason why none of them could say anything—even I—in response to Mellie's outburst was quite simply that it was true, true as blue and all the way through.

The Martians wanted her.

And I was down among the dead men, boys and girls.

CHAPTER THIRTY-FOUR
THE BLACKENED SPINE OF PSARA

On the blackened spine of Psara,
Glory, pacing alone,
Broods on her shining heroes;
She crowns her hair with a band
Born from the spare, few grasses
That are left in the ruined land.
—Dionysios Solomos

ALEX SMITH, 5 BI-NOVEMBER, MARS YEAR VII
ISIS STATION, PLANET MARS

My shame is that I ran away. I left that meeting without saying another damned word, hearing Becky calling to me behind my back, and dearest Mellie crying out at my abandonment of her plight. But I couldn't face the idea of her going away into that alien environment for God knows how long, and so I ran off.

I fled for what seemed to me hours and hours, although I really don't know how much time actually passed. The sirens were silent, both internally and externally, so the Martians were leaving us alone for awhile.

What was I to do?

What *could* I do?

I finally wound up at the end of one long tunnel in the storage lockers, and there I located a hiding place to nurture my depression and distress. It was dark in there, and dark too in my soul, and I found some minor comfort in the two coincidences of conformity.

What was I to do?

I'd been coming to this pass for a very long time. My sins were finally catching up with me. I had lied and cheated and even killed to reach this point in my life. How many of the alien buggers had I slaughtered down below? No wonder they wouldn't answer me anymore.

I pulled the blackness in around me and brooded for a very long time, and then I fell asleep, wonder of wonders, and I dreamed again.

And it seemed to me that I saw Big Guy dressed as a croupier at a casino, dealing out cards to everyone seated at the table (his tentacles gave him an amazing dexterity). I looked down at my hand and I saw five jokers staring back at me. They started laughing.

"What's so funny?" I asked.

"You are," they said.

"I don't mean to be funny."

"That's why you are!"

Big Guy dealt me another board, a tarot card this time. It was the Hanged Man. He was swinging upside down back and forth on his gibbet.

"What's it all about?" I asked.

"Beats the hell out of me," the Hanged Man said.

Then I awoke.

I knew what I had to do. This particular building was located on the northern edge of the station. I headed to one of the airlocks, and found several spare environmental suits and masks and boots and similar gear. I sealed up completely to protect myself against the elements and radiation. In the process of stripping off my outerwear, I found a note stuffed in one of my pockets, something that I hadn't put there myself. I opened it up. It read:

Dr. Smith:

You've always doubted my abilities. I forgive you for this. You don't know what a burden they've been to me. What you've experienced with the Martians, I've had to deal with all my life.

I know where you're going. I know what you want to do. I can't help you, except to say this: don't believe everything you see or hear. They shadow things sometimes, and they have the power to cloud men's souls. They like the color red. They don't like green. They like bitter fruit. They don't taste anything sweet. They think alike. They feel differently. They're individuals. They're a group. Ultimately, they're not like you and me, not even close. Yet, I believe communication between our species is still possible.

May God walk with you on your path.

Nomsah V.

I was almost as stunned as when my daughter Mellie had made her announcement. So much of my world was based on fantasies of my own creation. But sometimes fantasies are all we have, and sometimes fantasies become real enough that they enable us—or force us—to do things that otherwise would be impossible.

I opened the airlock door and stepped out in the roaring gale. The blast of high wind almost blew me off my feet, despite the thin atmospheric pressure. The cold, sand-filled zephyr nearly killed my resolve. Then I remembered why I was here, and who would walk in my place if I didn't do this thing. So I went out—and I went on.

Maybe that's what life is all about in the end. Despite the constant setbacks, despite the sorrow and pain and sense of continual loss, despite everything, you just go on, because the alternative is a diminution of what it means to be human. This is our definition as a race: we never give up. We keep picking ourselves up off the ground and going forward. We don't accept failure. The blackened spine of Psara, all that was left of the inhabitants of that doomed Greek island, simply spurred the few survivors to seek justice and retribution against the invaders.

So I walked out into the night, determined to face the Martians once and for all, determined to get the answers that all of us so desperately needed, *including* the aliens, if they only knew that. Perhaps Big Guy *did* know it. Maybe it saw something there. Maybe they vitally needed something from us to remain viable as a continuing entity on this planet.

I just opened my mind and let the droning sound, the static of the æther, fill the recesses of my head.

"Come on, Big Guy!" I huffed out under my puffy breath. "Come and get me, if you want me!"

And damned if they didn't!

CHAPTER THIRTY-FIVE
SOME CRAVEN SCRUPLE

Some craven scruple
Of thinking too precisely on the event.
—William Shakespeare

ALEX SMITH, 5 BI-NOVEMBER, MARS YEAR VII
UNKNOWN LOCATION, PLANET MARS

I strode forward as boldly as I could in a 150-MPH gale, with no idea of where I was headed or how I'd get there. I just trusted in our "keepers" to reel me in, if they wanted me. I had to watch every step, though, or risk being knocked down by the unruly wind, and rolled right over the ground like a tumbleweed. I kept my head down and just bulled my way through.

It didn't take long for the physical and mental stress to bring my inherent weakness back, together with the pressure in my chest and lungs. I ignored it. I'd either go forward or I'd die. I felt the same as when I'd confronted the great strider in Golden Gate Park in San Francisco a dozen years earlier.

To hell with it all!

"Take me or not, you little buggers," I gasped. "Just don't point fingers at me any longer."

Eventually I saw the main gate of our compound looming in front of me. Amazingly, it was standing wide open. There was no sign of the guards who should have been stationed there. They were probably all hunched down in their bunkers on either side of the opening. I just ambled on through.

Further out I had to bypass the wreckage of a strider intermingled with that of a burned-out half-track. The body of a Martian lay strewn across the corpse of a man. Is this what we'd come to, finally? Was there no commonality left to us except killing each other? Surely there had to be something more. Surely we could find some middle ground, couldn't we, Big Guy?

On and on and on I trod, placing one weary foot in front of another, wishing that the damnable wind would just go away and leave me in peace, wishing that I had nothing left to do. At times I had to stop to catch my breath; the intervals were becoming more and more frequent, and I knew that I would collapse for good on one of these occasions.

Where were the Martians?

Oh, that eternal cry of lamentation to the Lord! We'd been asking ourselves that question ever since we'd landed on this godforsaken world, and we still had no real answer.

Where were the Martians?

"Where *are* you buggers, eh? Come and get me!" I screamed into the gibbering gale. "What's the matter with you all: caterpillar got your tongue?"

I started laughing out loud at the notion, and then began coughing heavily. I had fluid in my lungs and my throat, and I couldn't seem to clear it. The damned breather kept interfering, so I yanked it off, just for a moment, and then it was jerked from my hand by a gust of wind. The thin, icy atmosphere of carbon dioxide couldn't even begin to sustain my life. I fumbled for my spare mask, but my fingers were numb, and I couldn't seem to make them work properly. I started to cry.

Goddam it, just give me a chance out here, I thought to myself. *Just give us a chance.*

But I had to breathe in finally, and when I did everything started going gray around the edges, and I fell to the ground, clutching at my aching throat and pounding heart. It felt like someone was sitting on my chest. The pressure just wouldn't let up, and I knew this wasn't going to end well.

And then I died.

When I finally came to myself again, I was riding in some kind of large vehicle. My clothes were gone, the air was warm and full of oxygen, and I was utterly alone. The car or whatever it was seemed to be self-sustaining. In the dim light of the Martian corridor, I could discern through the single domed window the occasional flash of a cross passage as we rushed by. Once we slowed almost to a crawl, and then veered right in a broad curve and eventually left again, when the machine revved up once more and began accelerating down the straightaway. I assumed that this dogleg had been created to bypass one of the areas that we'd bombed the previous month.

There was a tube of the sweet liquid on the floor next to me, so I opened it and sipped the wonderful nectar. I could feel the energy returning to my abused body. Bruises were beginning to form everywhere on my skin. Strangely, though, my heart seemed sound again, and my lungs were clear. Maybe I was dreaming after all.

Abruptly the domed vehicle began to slow, and eventually wound to a gentle stop. The top popped open on one side and I climbed out. As soon as I was clear of the machine, it closed itself up again, and continued on down that endless Martian tunnel.

It had left me standing nude near a smaller connecting corridor. I glanced up and saw at once that the ceiling lights were flickering off in that direction, so I slowly shuffled my way into the new passage. I noticed at once a change in the illumination. For some reason that I couldn't fathom, the light glowed here a pale pink, not yellow, as was often the case elsewhere. Then I remembered what Madame Stavroula had said: the Martians liked the color red.

As I came around a bend, I suddenly was confronted by a group of the alien bipeds, whom I'd called the monkey-creatures when we'd had our little *tête-à-tête* with them the previous month. They'd proven themselves to be savage and utterly fearless warriors, and they brandished their primitive weapons at me now, crowding in on all sides. I had no choice but to go along with them or be killed.

We walked for miles. Eventually, I tried to stop for a few moments, but they wouldn't let me rest there. They kept jabbering and jabbing at me with their spears, finally picking me up and carrying me along on their shoulders. The monkey-bipeds were frail creatures, really, and I still don't know how they were able to tote a full-sized man without using some kind of stretcher—but this was the second time that this happened.

Eventually we entered a huge cavern lined with their nests. A beautiful lake occupied the right-hand section of the room, but to the left was a platform on which sat a biped adorned with an elaborate headdress and garments. It motioned me forward, and then began gibbering at me with its chit-chit-chit sounds. I had no idea what they meant.

When it realized that I didn't understand what it was saying, it spoke to one of my bearers, who crawled up to its leader and bowed its head down before it. The king or whatever it was stabbed the bearer with its spear, and watched dispassionately as the thing breathed its last breath in front of us.

Then it pointed at me, and pointed again at the dead body of its subject. Suddenly I realized that it was telling me that I had killed some of its fellow monkey-creatures, which was, of course, perfectly true. I had the impression that it only cared about the issue because it had not given me permission to do this.

It chittered at another minion, who brought forth a tablet and handed it to me. I couldn't make any sense out of the thing at first. The slate consisted of upright lines grouped together in series of twelve. Then I understood that this represented the grand sum of all of the dead monkey-folk that I had personally been responsible for. The leader waved a hand at me in the universal gesture of, "What do *you* think?"

I handed it back to the attendant without comment.

Then the monarch said something else, and my arms were seized again. I was pushed and carried over to the main platform, where a kind of syringe attached to a gourd was stuck in my ass, and a bottle of my blood was efficiently and quickly and painfully extracted. This was handed to the monkey-king, who held it up and showed it to me.

A great chorus of chitters erupted from the audience.

The leader took back the slate, and pointedly erased one upright line. The creature then gave it back to me, and when I tried to return the thing, it bared its teeth at me and growled. I now understood my penalty.

The monkey-folk paid their dues in blood to their Martian overlords, or whatever they were to them. I would now recompense them for the lost vital fluids that I'd generated by killing 212 of their fellow creatures—and I'd stay down here until that was accomplished, however long it took. I had sinned most grievously in their eyes, and I would now pay the price, over and over and over again, until the reckoning was balanced once more.

I would become a veritable blood bank for these primitives.

Then they took me to a very nice but bare room where they treated me with food and drink—need to keep the prisoner fattened up!—and gave me a hard pallet on which to sleep. The loss of blood and the loss of innocence soon claimed me that night. My craven scruples had finally caught up with me.

"Oh, Smith," I said, "you've done it again!"

CHAPTER THIRTY-SIX
MUSKETAQUID

There's no rood has not a star above it.
—Ralph Waldo Emerson

ALEX SMITH, (?) BI-NOVEMBER, MARS YEAR VII
UNKNOWN LOCATION, PLANET MARS

I dreamed of Musketaquid, "the place where the water flows through the grasses" in Emerson's poem of that title. Only here the grass had been replaced by the red weed, which waved back and forth in the breeze like the locks of some mad Medusa, the tips of the plants giving rise to the caterpillar creatures that I'd viewed during my previous trip to the Martian underground.

I realized then, even through the fog of my befuddled mind, that all life on Mars was interconnected, that this vision of mine was not just some fantasy created by an overactive id or imagination. The linkage was real.

And then, half asleep, half awake, I remembered eating the weed in the distress of my starvation back on Earth during the War of Two Worlds. It was the nature of the Martian flora and fauna to integrate with other forms of life. This was the alien way of existence. Nothing dwelled in isolation on Mars—it literally couldn't! To survive the eons with so little water and so few resources, the biosphere on this planet had evolved into a finely refined collaboration of interrelated genomes and fecundity. Everything contributed to everything else. Everything was ultimately recycled.

Even me!

The days flowed together, one into another, and I gave, oh I gave, of my vital resources to the monkey-creatures, one gourd at a time. It got so bad that they had to start looking for additional places in which to poke me. My veins collapsed after a week or two, and my right arm in particular became one long mass of purple-and-black bruises. Once they had to stick me in between my fingers in order to draw blood, which was no fun at all. They were not inherently gentle beings.

I lost track of time completely. Without a chronometer I had no way of registering the passage of the hours, but I think that several weeks had passed before I was brought again to Big Guy, the largest of the squid-like intelligent Martians whom I'd met during my previous visit.

The meeting went much as before.

Sometime during one of my sleep cycles I was carried unconscious to another compartment in the underground complex, and there placed on a table in a laboratory. When I awoke, I was already surrounded by Big Guy and its compatriots, including Crook Mouth, whom I recognized from our one previous encounter.

"Hi-i, g-guys!" I croaked out.

I was completely immobilized. One of the biped attendants was busily attaching various electrodes to my body. Wonder of wonders, they used suction cups, just like in our own medical facilities. The pervading odor was different, however, a vague fishy smell that I'd come to associate with the giant tentacle-folks.

"So, what's on the agenda today?" I asked.

No response, of course.

Crook Mouth rumbled something at one of the monkey-creatures, and it turned on a large machine standing off to one side. I felt a little tingle, nothing more, and then I began hearing a shu-shunk noise emanating from the device, over and over again; and I realized suddenly that it was the machine-amplified beating of my own heart.

Crook Mouth turned around and pointed with one of its tentacles to something on the instrument, but my head was held immobile staring straight up at the ceiling, and I couldn't make out what they were peering at so intently over there.

Crook Mouth fiddled with something else, and then one of the bipeds twisted a dial on another machine, and the fingers on my black-and-blue right arm began twitching up and down, one after another. It was positively unnerving, if you don't mind the pun. They did the same tests on other parts of my body, evidently trying to figure out how everything fit together. They didn't miss anything, spending what I thought was an inordinate amount of time focused on the appendage dangling between my legs, which must have been unique to them, since all of them reproduced asexually (so I believed).

Then they withdrew for a time, while one of the attendants fed me some of that nectar of theirs from a tube.

An hour or so later, they were back again, examining the organs on my head in great detail. Then something very curious happened. Big Guy bent over me with its huge, hairless body, and carefully attached a half dozen of its tentacles to either side of my skull. One by one the other Martian squid-folk carefully followed suit, using just one of their limbs to reach out and touch me—or Big Guy.

For an instant, just for a moment, I felt like I was falling down this long, lonely shaft, losing myself forever in the dim, dark recesses of a great cavern at the bottom; and shining all around the edges of the blackness were the reflected orbs of the great Martian eyes, all staring back at me, penetrating my very soul. The walls of the cave suddenly expanded outwards, growing ever greater even as I watched; and the number of brooding eyes examining my persona multiplied and multiplied until they were legion.

The thought of being forever without privacy, of being immersed in this cauldron of cohabitation for all eternity, overwhelmed me.

I started screaming, "Noooooooo!" and tried to pull back, but they wouldn't let me go.

My fear increased in geometric proportion as the number of outside observers continued to grow. Then Big Guy abruptly released me, and I was myself again, gasping for air, terrified of what I had seen.

One by one, the alien experimenters withdrew.

The attendants injected me with something, and I felt my body sliding away from me. I was left to sleep the sad sleep of the maimed and the exhausted.

I dreamed again of Musketaquid, "the place where the water flows through the grasses," and my sanity was gradually restored.

When I awoke, I was a blood bank again.

CHAPTER THIRTY-SEVEN
A GAME OF CHESS

The chess board is the world,
the pieces are the phenomenon of the universe,
the rules of the game are what we call the laws of Nature.
The player on the other side is hidden from us.
—Thomas Henry Huxley

ALEX SMITH, (?) BI-NOVEMBER, MARS YEAR VII
UNKNOWN LOCATION, PLANET MARS

For some unknown period I continued to be the primary donor of my vital fluids to the six-foot-tall creatures I called the monkey-folk, one of several intelligent species dwelling on Mars. I was never actually sure how many of the plants or animals I encountered did possess some form of sentience—or indeed, whether they all had at least a modicum of mental congruity. Their biological interdependence suggested other points of correlation, but I leave such speculations to the exo- or xeno-biologists and -botanists among us.

Beyond my hemo-subservience to the creatures, I was left pretty much on my own. They fed me regularly—it was very much in their interest to do so—and they made sure that I didn't wander too far apace, but beyond such considerations, I was left to explore the strange new worlds and indubitably interesting civilizations that I encountered "Down Under" (indeed, I was tempted to baptize the whole area the Ellisonian Fields).

I saw many more of the Martian "bugs" and the other smaller critters than we could reasonably have expected to find, dozens of them; and I encountered many strange and bizarre fungi and flora inhabiting the specially tended gardens and arboreta. Most of the actual labor to maintain these facilities appeared to be handled by the bipeds. They in turn gained much of their sustenance, apparently, from some fish-like creatures inhabiting the lakes attached to their nests, devouring the swimmers' flesh in a fashion that we would regard as traditional, although they ate everything raw. However, I also saw them eat several of the caterpillar-creatures and at least one example of a kind of slug that looked like a cross between a worm and a very large green grub.

As I've previously stated, my observations convinced me that everything that I saw on Mars was interdependent and interrelated, from the greatest of the creatures (the intelligent squid-folk) to the smallest (an insect about the size of the nail on my fourth finger; it looked a little like a red ladybug without wings).

I don't know how days many passed before I was taken again to see Big Guy. All I know is that I awoke in its presence in what appeared to be its private quarters, although I didn't and still don't know this for a fact. It's possible that the aliens lived communally, as did every other species that I noted on Mars. This room could just as easily have been the Martian's equivalent of an office or workspace. There's so much that we don't understand about the critters.

Big Guy was sitting or lying in one corner of the place in a recessed pool of some kind, the water bubbling around it, several of its tentacles draped idly over the tiled rim of the basin. One of the reasons why I thought that this might be a private facility is the copious decoration that I saw displayed everywhere.

Even the floor was patterned in colorful stone scrolling and sparkling geometric designs. The work was beautifully done and very well accomplished to a high level of both skill and artistry. There was a marvelously arranged garden near the entranceway, filled with exotic flowers and bulbs and gourds, some of them giving off extraordinarily subtle odors, although a few smelled like a pail full of dead fish. At least one of these blooms spanned several feet in diameter.

I also noticed what appeared to be some *objets d'art* displayed on a low table along one wall. These included a highly polished piece of wood, what I think was a fossil, and several artifacts that I couldn't place at all. They looked utterly foreign to the Martian culture that I'd seen, and they certainly hadn't derived from Earth. There was also something that took my breath away: a gold aureus of the Roman Emperor Vespasian, his fat provincial face staring out at me from the obverse side of the coin. I wondered if the unidentifiable pieces similarly derived from off-world sites.

One of the biped attendants entered the room and prostrated itself before the Martian. It touched its head to the tile and crossed its arms behind its back. Then it lifted itself up, stuck out its tongue, and received a small drop of something directly from the squid-creature's mouth. The look of ecstasy that passed over the monkey-man's face was astonishing.

It turned around and presented to Big Guy what on Earth would have been its anus. The Martian exuded its feeding-tube, inserted it in the place meant for it, and drank. It too took on the expression of a drug addict, its eyes glazing over and rolling up in its huge head, and a large *"ahhh-hoo"* exhaling from its lungs.

This completely destroyed the picture that I had already erected in my mind concerning the relationship between these two species. Obviously, both sides gave and gained something from these periodic feedings.

Then Big Guy finished its "snack," withdrew its tube, and the attendant backed out of the room, properly deferential in its incessant bowing, presumably to repeat the ritual at some later date.

"So why am I here, Aroostook?" I asked.

The alien paid no attention to me whatever.

"Aroostook!" I said again, but this time I tried to envision the

Martian in my mind while speaking its name verbally.

Abruptly it looked directly at me.

"Sah-Mit!" it rasped in its gravelly voice.

Then it reached out a tentacle and gave the universal gesture of "Come hither!"

I got up and walked over to the front of the basin, where I squatted on the ground a few feet away. I'd never before had the occasion to focus on one of the Martians so closely.

For the first time, I noticed that its skin was not exactly smooth, as I'd imagined, but rather bumpy; and that there were even patterns to the gray that hadn't been visible at a distance. The eyes of the thing were supremely intelligent. I couldn't tell whether or not they were sympathetic. I do believe that the alien was a leader of some sorts to its people, and that like most leaders, was a political animal.

"Sah-Mit!" it said again.

I paid more attention.

It reached out one of its tentacles, and I thought that it was about to touch me, but it actually stopped short, and pointed down at one of the tiles between us. I looked more closely at the *tableau*, and realized that there was a large red stone and a large green stone laid side by side just in front of the basin rim. Both were round and completely different from any of the other rocks that had been placed in the immediate vicinity.

"Sah-Mit!" it said again, thumping its tentacle on the red stone.

"Yes," I said, "I am Sah-Mit," and I imagined an image of myself in my own mind.

I actually thought the bugger smiled at me, but it was probably my imagination working overtime.

Then it pointed back at itself and said, "Ah-Roohs-Tookh."

I touched the red tile, which meant, I think, "yes" or "good" or "true" or something like that, compared with the opposite value for the green stone.

It tapped me on the forehead and said, "Ah-Roohs-Tookh."

I jabbed my finger smartly onto the green tile, trying to

dampen my elation. It was surely the most primitive form of communication, but goddam it, we were finally talking to each other!

The challenge was to frame my questions in such a way as to elicit a meaningful response from the Martian.

"Why am I here, Aroostook?" I asked, making an interrogatory in my mind.

No response: too general.

"My wife, Becky"—her portrait displayed in the front of my mind—"alive?"—I made her form run to and fro.

Red tile: "Yes."

"My daughter, Mellie: alive?"

The same.

"The Isis Station: intact?"

"Yes."

"Granick Valley Station: intact?"

"No."

"Can we live together?"—I depicted the Martians and humans, tentacle and hand intertwined.

Red tile and green tile both: "Maybe."

"Who are you?"—I put Big Guy in front of a crowd of other Martians.

No response: either it didn't know what I was asking, or it didn't want to answer, or there was no answer that I could understand.

"Truce?"—I showed the striders withdrawing from Isis Station.

"Maybe."

"What do you want?"—I imagined myself handing an empty basket to Aroostook, combined with an interrogatory.

No response, but the alien barked out a guttural command, and one of the biped attendants immediately appeared from somewhere, holding a slate in its hands and what appeared to be a piece of light rock. These it gave to its master, who took them and began sketching something on the solid surface of the pad. After a moment, it turned it over and showed me what it had drawn: the face of my daughter Mellie.

"No!" I screamed, stabbing my finger down on the green tile. "No!"

"My child"—I imagined the girl as a bud coming off my back.

"Yes," the alien immediately agreed, but then pointed back to itself and once again stabbed the red stone, obviously saying that Mellie was *its* child as well.

"No!" I emphasized, stabbing down at the emerald rock over and over again; but it kept responding with the red one.

For a moment we were both silent, facing off with each other, the gulf of misunderstanding or disagreement looming between us and threatening to damn both of our races to the hell of war. The Martian was as stubborn as I. Finally it gave a great sigh, quite audibly so, and burped another command at the monkey-creature who was serving it.

The biped left the room and returned a moment later, holding in its arms the small figure of a young Martian, barely six inches in diameter. It seemed somewhat distorted to me, but since I'd never actually seen one of the alien young, beyond the half-formed bud that had been reported from the original invasion back on Earth, I really didn't know what to expect. Maybe they changed remarkably in appearance as they aged. I suspected that Big Guy was the oldest of the creatures that I'd yet met, and that increasing size was somehow a function of both antiquity and authority—and in this I was later proven correct.

"Sah-Mit!" Aroostook barked at me.

I looked over at it.

The Martian pointed at the young one, and said, "Sah-Roohs-Tookh."

"Your child?" I envisioned in my mind, showing it budding off the great back of the alien.

"Yes," it said.

Then it pointed a tentacle at me, and my blood froze in my veins.

"No," I said, "I don't want your child. I'm not interested in an exchange."

I showed it images of me with my child, and him with his.

It took the slate, wiped it clean, and then drew something else, handing the finished picture to me. It was obviously intended to be a family portrait. It depicted me and Becky and "Buddy," the child.

"No," I said, flattered that it considered giving me its child to raise, but not wanting the honor, now or in the future, not if it meant leaving Mellie to the mercy of these cold-hearted creatures.

You see, I really wasn't getting it yet. I was thinking, as my wife would say, in the box, and not at all like the aliens.

I could almost see the frustration written across Big Guy's face. It wasn't communicating exactly what it meant, and it knew it, so it tried once more.

Again the slate was washed clean (actually, it sprayed the thing, if you want to know the truth, splattering me in the process), and then it frantically began scratching a new portrait on the piece of black stone, scribbling furiously with its tentacle. It thrust the result into my stomach, causing me to lose my breath briefly.

I looked down at the thing. I couldn't help myself, and I couldn't forget what I saw there.

"No, no, no, no, no!" I screamed.

"Sah-Mit!"

The alien's voice cut through my turmoil.

It stabbed its finger down at the red tile, and I knew then that it was true. The picture that Big Guy had drawn for my behalf, had scratched on the slate in order to enlighten me of the reality of the situation, displayed a human being—the portrait was unmistakably *moi*—with Buddy jutting out of my back.

The baby Martian looked up at me from the arms of its attendant. Then it cried out in its high-pitched voice. I didn't understand it at first, because it sounded so much different from Big Guy. Suddenly and appallingly I realized what it was trying to say:

"Smith!"

CHAPTER THIRTY-EIGHT
BID TIME RETURN

O! Call back yesterday, bid time return.
—William Shakespeare

ALEX SMITH, 31 JANUARY, MARS YEAR VIII
DOWN UNDER, ELLISONIAN FIELDS, PLANET MARS

This is the way the world ends, not with bang but a whimper. And this is the way my story ends as well.

Over time I was able to convince Aroostook or Big Guy to allow me to bring Becky with me to live Down Under beneath Utopia Planitia with our daughter and my quasi-son, Buddy. My blood had been employed for several purposes other than sustenance, it seems, and it had nourished more than one event for the Martian scientists, who were happy indeed to have the weed-tainted Earthman's fluids on which to experiment. Or so I surmised, because our communications skills still left a whole lot to be desired.

Becky was appalled when she discovered the truth of the situation.

"You've got to be kidding," she said.

I think she actually considered leaving me then, but when she realized that any possible settlement with the aliens depended, at least in their minds, on having Mellie readily available to them, she finally came around.

Of course, I still have many unanswered questions remaining, and they all really boil down to one thing.

Why?

Why did they declare war in the first place?

Why did they attack us?

Why did they all die on Earth?

Why did they decide to negotiate with us on Mars?

Why, why, why?

And when I framed these interrogatories as best I could to Aroostook, who is, by the way, the only individual among the aliens who has allowed us to deal with it on a personal level, it didn't respond.

And then I had to ask again, because I wasn't at all certain *why* it didn't respond.

You see, I just have a suspicious mind by nature, and I can't believe in the Tooth Fairy any more. I also remembered what Madame Stavroula told me before my second descent into the Martian underworld.

(By the way, they would never have anything to do with poor Nomsah, nothing whatever, and again I'm not sure as to the reason. I suspect that Nomsah would have gained far too much in any exchange, and they didn't and don't want us to know certain things.)

I wonder sometimes who's really in charge on Mars, if anyone is. You see, there were situations that I've observed where the tall bipeds appeared to be calling the shots, and at least once when I thought that the furtive little ferret-creatures, who were rarely visible to me, demanded and got their way.

Then too, I spotted something the other day that profoundly disturbed me. I was visiting with Big Guy when it abruptly turned away from me and concentrated its vision on the far wall. I think it was receiving a mental communication of some kind. It waved me off, and when I didn't move fast enough, grunted a command to the monkey-creatures, who promptly grabbed my arms and hauled me away.

But as I left, I glimpsed something that I obviously hadn't been intended to see. It was another kind of squid-creature, differently shaped about its upper body, and with a pure white hue to its skin. I actually think that there were more of them hovering in the background.

So if the Martians have different races or varieties, if that's what they are, how do they interact?

I asked Big Guy about the White Martians, but it wouldn't reply—again!

I then asked it who was going to win the World Series this year, the Cubs or the Yankees, and it said the Cubs! Pfui! Maybe the aliens do have a sense of humor. Was it toying with me, or was it making an honest reply?

* * * * * * *

This is how the worlds sorted themselves out:

The Martians promptly withdrew from Isis Station, and left it unmolested thereafter.

Granick Valley had mostly been destroyed during the alien attack, but we rescued about fifty survivors from the ruins, including Father Phil, who was highly taken with Reverend Lesley. We also salvaged some additional supplies from Granick; the Martians let us scrounge there without interference. They made it clear, however, that we could never rebuild that base again.

Big Guy drew a map for me. It depicted Isidis Planitia with the small image of a human standing in the middle. It then drew a line across the end of the plain, separating it from Utopia Planitia, and put the figure of a Martian just north of the line.

Isidis was our sphere of control, it was saying, but north of that boundary everything else was theirs.

They built a station right at the border of our two territories, and that's where we met when we wanted to talk.

Becky, Mellie, and I set up housekeeping in our own series of rooms in the underground caverns near the residence or office of Aroostook. We were given our own set of attendants, which I suspect was a high honor indeed in Martian society—or it may simply just have been their way of controlling the unruly humans living among them.

We had frequent visitors from the surface, including Mindon, Zee, Andrews, Markus, Alexander, and Scott; but no military types or female Sensitives were allowed to join us.

Isis Station was restored, and soon became almost completely self-sufficient, thanks to copious assistance from the aliens, who provided new sources of water, together with food that was quite edible by our kind, and even a bit tasty. I wondered if some of these things had been genetically engineered to make them more palatable to our gullets.

I did warn our people, of course, of the possible consequences of eating the Martian plants, but most of my compatriots didn't seem too bothered by the idea, other than Burgess and his staff, who would never touch them.

The aliens also terminated the great sandstorm in very short order, winding it down within a week or so of our "agreement." How they'd generated the hurricane in the first place remains a great mystery, but also a kind of warning: such power vastly exceeds our own control of the environment, even on our home planet, much less on Mars; and what the aliens have done once, they can accomplish again, if they choose.

The bombardment of Earth by asteroids ceased quite abruptly. How this was done is unknown, except that one of our observatories did record an explosion somewhere out in the space between the orbit of the Red Planet and our world.

Who are the Martians?

I don't have any certain answers to that question. I think they're supremely intelligent beings. I think they're caring beings. I think they're political beings, and I think that we don't really know very much about them, even today—and that we still need to learn a great deal more.

I'm the one person among the entire human race who has had—and, I hope, will continue to have—the opportunity to view the aliens at close range over a long period of time. It bothers me that I don't understand sometimes what Big Guy is about. I wonder what that creature really thinks of us, if it even considers things in those terms. I do have the distinct impression that they all regard us as inferior beings.

Where do we go from here?

I hope that we can discover some peaceful coexistence together. I know that our military godfathers are still planning to bring another expedition in two years (one Martian cycle) to the planet of the ancient God of War, including more complements of advanced weaponry. I think this is a mistake, and I've told them so, for all the good it's done. As a direct result, I'm now *persona non grata* in certain parts of Isis Station, whenever I visit there.

Tomorrow is the First of February, and I wanted to finish my account before passing into a new month. So much has changed over the years—I've changed—and I actually look forward to the discoveries that we'll all make together in this brave new future of ours. I hope that it develops better than it started.

Becky and I have reconciled our differences. She's become much more interested in the Martian culture, and her insights into the alien life often surpass my own.

But the wonder for both of us is the development of our daughter Mellie, whose interactions with the world underground have been both delightful and amazing. Contrary to my expectations, she hasn't been harmed or probed or hassled in any way by Big Guy and its compatriots.

And as for Buddy, well I've grown rather fond of the little bugger. I don't know how much of my blood runs in his veins, but it's obvious that he's learning how to talk with us in a way that his bud-brothers never will—and perhaps that's exactly why he was made the way he was. I think of him as a "he," even though he's probably no more sexual in orientation than any of the rest of them—although who knows, really? He's always underfoot, but he's growing fairly rapidly at this stage, and learning new things prodigiously. He and my daughter have become fast friends, which is one of the things that the Martians obviously intended.

So tomorrow we celebrate the passage of another month, as we celebrated the turn of the new year a few weeks earlier. I've become nostalgic in my old age, although I'm not really that old in Earth terms—I've just lived a lot. Min is coming by and so is Zee and so is Nomsah (by permission of Big Guy), and a few of the others to whom we feel close. Ha, I even invited Reverend Lesley, whose first name, I just recently discovered, is Marion—I heard Father Phil referring to a "Marion" the other day, and had no idea about whom he was talking until he explained a few things (the birds and the bees) to me.

When I think back on the days before the Martians came to Earth, there are occasions when I want to say "Call back yesterday, bid time return," in the words of the Immortal Bard. It all seems so long ago now, such a different, even alien, time and environment. My years at the University are another life indeed. Some other person did those things, some other individual taught those students and served on committees and published books on *The Future of Man*.

Now I'm *living* the future of man, or at least what I *think* will become our future, in conjunction with the Martians. In the words of Paul Valéry, *"Le vent se lève, il faut tenter de vivre"*— "The wind is rising, but we must attempt to live."

I asked Big Guy today if there was life elsewhere in the universe. I painted a picture in my mind of the stars with creatures walking among them.

Its tentacle tapped solidly down on the red tile.

"Have you met them?" I asked.

No answer.

I wonder.

I truly wonder.

CHAPTER THIRTY-NINE
THE GRAND ILLUSION

The wind and clouds,
Now here, now there.
—John Clare

AH-ROOHS-TOOKH, FIRST BUD OF THE 3,892ND CYCLE
Day 368,221,059,712

May you know your way! May the many be One!

The furry things remain a difficulty. They think not as Unity. They feel not the sorrow. They know not the wisdom. The joy is absent in their lives. Yet, still they are here.

We see their minds. We do not understand them as units. They cannot think as One. The being called Sah-Mit tries to find the way. There are impediments.

We see their minds:

DR. MINDON MIN

Alex has gone all native on us. I visited him and his family Down Under, as he calls it, and it scared the holy shit out of me. Man, here was this mini-alien running all over the place on its tentacles, beeping and yelling and even laughing, which I'd never heard the Marties do before. Smith said it was his son, Buddy! I mean, I always thought that I had an open mind and all back on Earth, but this is too much.

The good news, though, is that Puff's coming out on Expedition IV. I finally decided that I'd better not wait any longer—who else'd put up with me, after all?—and I'm not the young Romeo I used to be. So I told her if she wanted me, well, I was hers for life. Boy, that's a big change, isn't it? All those ladies back on Earth will think I've been bewitched by the Martians. Man, I haven't, really. They haven't had any effect on me at all. Honestly.

Warp speed, hon!

CORP. ZELBERT "ZEE" ZWINGLI

Baghdad: a car bomb blowing up al-Jazirah Café, two of my buddies shredded, 120-degree heat and no power, the people hating us all, all, all the uncertainty of life. Oh, yeah, I recall every fuckin' minute.

People think cuz I speak bad I can't think good. They don't know. They don't know me at all. Only *they* understand. Only *they* see the real me. I can't let anyone else see. If they knew the pain in me, they would put me away. Only *they* accept me for what I am.

But can *I* accept *them* for what *they* are?

Huh? Huh? *Huh?*

We're having asparagus today, fresh and green and with a little melted margarine and coarse pepper. Green is good.

THE VERY REVEREND CAPTAIN MARION LESLEY

The Martians are the evil ones condemned to eternal damnation by the Almighty and Merciful Lord God Jesus. If we have truck with them, we lower ourselves to their abomination. They should be exterminated with prejudice, each and every one.

Father Phil came by today. I really think he's an upstanding Christian gentleman, and very knowledgeable in the ways of the Lord. He has a degree in theology from Claremont. Isn't that simply wonderful? I thought that I would miss Earth, and I did for awhile, but now everything is different. This is home now. This is my new ministry. I must save our boys from the gray devils in tentacles.

God bless us all, each and every one.

MAJOR GENERAL FLEMING THOMAS "FRITZ" BURGESS

Just received word from Space Force Command that the new bomb has been tested on the far side of the Moon, where it couldn't be observed by the enemy. This one'll send its radiation right down into the ground, destroying all life to a depth of a thousand feet. They tell me they'll have the finished product in time to include on E-IV.

Smith continues to be difficult. I've asked him to report to me on a regular basis with descriptions of the Martian emplacements and military strength, but he says he's through with such things now, and that we ought to be looking for ways to work with the aliens.

They're not like us. It's us vs. them. We destroy them or they destroy us. We're fighting for the same thing. Only one of us'll survive. Next time *we'll* win. We've got to.

MADAME STAVROULA (NOMSAH VASSILIDIS)

I see too much.

MS. MÉLUSINE ELIZABETH "MELLIE" SMITH

I like Mars. I wish more of my friends could visit me down here. Buddy is fun. I miss our games. Daddy got me an uplink the other day. That helps. Big Guy says I'm the key to their future. That's nice, but....

CORPSMAN JAY C. ROBINSON, PHOBOS BASE

The General asked me what I'd found.

"Well, sir," I said, "It's actually a simple carrier code. I cracked it right away. Shall I play it for you?"

I put it on speaker: it went: *"Ooh-lah"* over and over again.

"Where's it coming from?" he asked.

"Dunno, sir. Can't pin it down. So far as I can tell, the whole planet's generating it."

"Where's it being sent?"

"That's why I called, sir. It's going to Earth."

AFTERWORD
"*INVASION!* — AND BEYOND"

It started in the Fall of 2004 with a phone call from Tim Underwood, Publisher of Underwood Books, whom I've known for thirty-five years or more. He was considering publishing an illustrated, coffee-table-style volume as a tie-in to the then forthcoming motion picture version of *War of the Worlds*— itself a very loose adaptation of the classic science-fiction novel by H. G. Wells—and wanted me to write the commentary. The project never developed, for a variety of reasons; and I've never viewed the Spielberg film, again for a variety of reasons.

Late in the Spring of 2005, Tim called me out of the blue, and asked me to do a rewrite of the second half of Wells's 1898 original novel, which Tim had already started recasting into a modern-day version set in the San Francisco Bay Area. I agreed, and quickly finished the job on a rush-rush basis. After seeing my work, he then asked me to revamp the entire book into one consistent, unified voice, and to use what I could of both his contribution and H. G.'s seminal work. Shortly thereafter, I proposed—and Tim agreed—that I pen two sequels to *War of Two Worlds*, as it was now called. These would be set some years after the action in the first novel, and would be entirely of my own devising.

The first two books in the sequence were announced for publication in the Fall of 2005. Covers were designed and orders solicited. I rewrote Volume One in its entirety, with an eye towards creating the sequels; and then promptly plunged into

Volume Two, *Operation Crimson Storm*, completing it at the end of July. The books were typeset and I approved the galleys. I also prepared a brief outline of Volume Three, which was due to be written and published the following year, depending on the sales of the first two.

Once again, however, fate intervened, and the titles never appeared as scheduled. Well, *c'est la vie*—I'd been paid an advance and I'd done the work, and my publisher *liked* my work, more to the point. Maybe the novels would eventually see the light of day in some other venue. Indeed, I've never yet penned a book that wasn't eventually released in some professional forum.

There the matter rested for several years. And then, early in 2007, I again heard from Tim, and he suggested that we do *all three novels* as an omnibus (mind you, *número tres* had yet to be written!). So, I reread and re-edited the first two books, to familiarize myself again with the material, and then wrote *The Martians Strike Back!* as the concluding volume to the trilogy. The books were published under a new title, *Invasion! Earth vs. the Aliens* later that year—to a resounding clap of silence from the critics.

When the three-in-one version was declared out-of-print in 2010, I asked Tim for a reversion of the rights, and decided to have the novels reissued in the way that they were originally intended to be published—as separate works. So here they are, released finally as individual fictions—but with the titles of the first novel and the series switched, at the urging of my publisher. I hope you enjoy their new incarnations.

* * * * * * *

H. G. Wells never wrote a sequel the *War of the Worlds*, but Garrett P. Serviss did, in a serialized newspaper epic called *Edison's Conquest of Mars* (1898). The great American inventor signs on as part of an expedition to the Red Planet to punish the Martians for their audacity in invading Earth.

Edison is, of course, successful in defeating the tentacled aliens, thus saving our home planet from the prospect of being overwhelmed once more at some future date. The story was finally issued in book form in 1947.

The thought that our injured pride, together with the prospect of further warfare, might prompt a military response against Mars seemed to me quite reasonable, *if it could be done*; but getting there was only half the battle, I believed.

We tend to picture other intelligent lifeforms as simulcra of human beings, just Good Old Boys (or Girls) doing their thing on (or to) Planet Earth. Many fictional aliens, in both book and film form, follow the pattern seen in *Men in Black* and its sequel: they're really just like us, except that they (belch, fart, excrete, whatever) in some odd or unusual way. They're "illegal aliens," instead of truly being otherworldly beings.

That has to be a vast oversimplication. Understanding other *humans* is difficult enough, as we witness constantly in our own lives and in our relationships with other countries around the globe. But to think that the creatures of *Avatar* (or any other example of modern science fiction) could be assimilated by our psyches so readily and easily is completely beyond reason. If we ever encounter a truly intelligent *alien* species, the problem from the very beginning will be finding a way to understand each other.

So, I fashioned my narrator, Alex Smith, as a man who's conflicted by the problem of communication—who's intelligent enough (unlike the military and political establishment of the story) to understand that communication *must* happen, if both species are to survive; but who has more than enough issues in just talking to his wife and friends, much less the Martians.

And yet he keeps on trying, as we all must.

Big Guy, the Martian elder and Smith's counterpart among the aliens, also keeps reaching out, perhaps for the same reasons (but since we never truly understand the inhabitants of the Red Planet, this is not really certain, as Smith himself is quick to admit).

None of the bridging attempts between cultures (or species) is easy—it never is. But I do think the book works on its own terms. It just poured out of my soul when I wrote it, which is usually a sign that I've tapped something very deep and very true (or perhaps, that I'm just spacing out on my own creativity!). I've had similar experiences with several other novels, and these kinds of books are alway a blast to write.

In any case, I hope you enjoy this new edition of *Operation Crimson Storm*, the very first separate publication of the novel in book form.

Robert Reginald
San Bernardino, California
23 February 2011

ABOUT THE AUTHOR

ROBERT REGINALD started writing as a child, and penned his first book during his senior year in college. He's been infected with terminal logorrhea ever since, churning out more than twelve million words of professional fiction and nonfiction. He settled in Southern California in 1969, where he served as an academic librarian for 40 years. He currently edits the Borgo Press Imprint of Wildside Press, and has also penned more than 120 published books and 13,000 short pieces.

His recent works of fiction include four Nova Europa historical fantasy novels, *The Dark-Haired Man; or, The Hieromonk's Tale* (2004), *The Exiled Prince; or, The Archquisitor's Tale* (2004), *Quæstiones; or, The Protopresbyter's Tale* (2005), and *The Fourth Elephant's Egg; or, The Hypatomancer's Tale* (forthcoming); two science-fiction novels, *Invasion!: Earth vs. the Aliens* (2007; a trilogy comprising *The War of Two Worlds*, *Operation Crimson Storm*, and *The Martians Strike Back!*) and *Knack' Attack: A Tale of the Human-Knacker War* (2010); two Phantom Detective mysteries, *The Phantom's Phantom* (2007) and *The Nasty Gnomes* (2008); a comic mystery, *The Paperback Show Murders* (2011); and three story collections, *Katydid & Other Critters: Tales of Fantasy and Mystery* (2001), *The Elder of Days: Tales of the Elders* (2010), and *The Judgment of the Gods and Other Verdicts of History* (2011).

Recent nonfiction works include an anthology, *Choice Words: The Borgo Press Book of Writers Writing About Writing* (2010); two collections, *Xenograffiti: Essays on Fantastic*

Literature (1996 & 2005) and *Classics of Fantastic Literature; or, Les Épines Noires* (with Douglas Menville, 2005); three guides to the Deryni world, *Codex Derynianus I* and *II* and *III* (with Katherine Kurtz, 1998 & 2005 & forthcoming); four histories, *San Quentin* (ed. with Bonnie Petry, 2005), *¡Viva California!: Seven Accounts of Life in Early California* (ed. with Mary Burgess, 2006), *The Eastern Orthodox Churches* (2005), and *The Coyote Chronicles: A Chronological History of California State University, San Bernardino, 1960-2010* (2010); a short autobiography, *Trilobite Dreams; or, The Autodidact's Tale* (2006); a cookbook, *Cal State Cooks* (ed. with Johnnie Ralph, 2006); and several bibliographies: *BP 300* (2007), *CSUSB Faculty Authors* (2006), *Murder in Retrospect* (with Jill Vassilakos, 2005), and *Draqualian Silk* (with William Maltese, 2010). In 1993 he received the Pilgrim Award from the Science Fiction Research Association. You can find him at:

http://www.millefleurs.tv

www.ingramcontent.com/pod-product-compliance
Lightning Source LLC
Chambersburg PA
CBHW020444270626
47155CB00022B/1456